Magic
in Suburbia

Elisabeth Waters

ISBN: 1-938185-00-5
ISBN-13: 978-1-938185-00-7

CONTENTS

TELL ME A STORY

Although I had been making jokes about the time warp for years, I never really believed in its existence until the night it grabbed me.

Anyone who knows me will tell you two things: (1) I claim to keep a time warp on my desk for losing important papers into, and (2) my house is so messy and disorganized that a time warp couldn't find anything in it either. My study is littered with the fallout of my thirty-year writing career—reference books on every available shelf and most flat surfaces, manuscripts slithering gracefully onto the floor, reams of paper stacked in odd corners, all covered with a dusting of paper clips, rubber bands, and pencil stubs—some days it's hard to find the typewriter. Add to this my absent-minded-professor husband and my two teenage children, and it's easy to see that a time warp would be quite superfluous. Well, it may be superfluous, but it's there.

It had been one of those days when everything went wrong. I was used to losing pens, pencils, typewriter ribbons, the odd ream of paper, and five-year-old manuscripts to the "time warp," but this afternoon I hadn't been able to find the manuscript I had been working on that morning. My husband informed me that I had misplaced it and it would turn up, my daughter assured me that the time warp would return it as soon as it finished reading it, and my son asked for an advance on his allowance. I wouldn't mind if the time warp would swallow my purse briefly at moments like that, but naturally the purse sat in plain sight on the kitchen table. My son would probably figure out a way to get it out of the time warp anyway. And, of course, once he got his advance, my daughter needed money for new shoes, and my husband was running out of lunch money. By the time I gave up and crawled up to bed I was considerably poorer—and I still couldn't find that darn manuscript!

I was dreaming, and I didn't know where I was. I woke up and sat up in bed to orient myself. I was in my own bed, my husband was snoring next to me and the clock on the bed table said 3:15 am. Then the numbers on the clock started flashing, the way they do after the power has been off, but instead of their usual 12:01 am, they were flashing numbers at random, and, while I was still wondering what was happening, nothingness picked me up and swallowed me.

It was the most horrible sensation—or rather, lack of sensation: I couldn't see anything but a sort of murky gray; I couldn't feel anything at all, not even air against my skin or moving through my lungs; I tried to scream and didn't make a sound, or if I did, I didn't hear it. I thought I must be mad, and then I heard the voice *inside* my head and I knew I was.

"Go on! What happens next?"

"What!?!" I still couldn't hear myself, but apparently the voice could. An image appeared in my mind of a page of manuscript, the last page I had written that morning. It stopped in mid-sentence.

"The story. What happens next?"

"Who are you?" At that point I didn't care what happened next in my story; I was more interested in what was going to happen next in my life. "Am I dead?"

"No, of course not. I'm 'the time warp you keep on your desk for losing important papers'—and that's unfair, I've never taken anything important, and I always return the stuff anyway. What happens next in the story?"

I'll say one thing for the time warp; it didn't get sidetracked easily. "How would I know what happens next? I haven't written it yet."

"Yes, you do know. How else could you write it? It's got to be in your mind. What happens next?"

"You're already in my mind. If it's there, why can't you find it for yourself?"

"Because it's in your subconscious, and I can't access that far down in your mind. I thought even writers knew that. What happens next?" It sounded like a child, nagging for yet another chapter of his bedtime story.

"I don't know. I can't access my subconscious either, not until I sit down at the typewriter and start typing." Something bumped against me in the gray murk. I reached out and ran my hands over it. It was my typewriter.

"What happens next?"

If it could act like a five-year-old, I could treat it like one. "Do your parents know that you're running around swallowing people and typewriters?"

"Well..." pause for thought, "they never said I couldn't!" it finished triumphantly.

I must be making progress; for the first time it hadn't said 'what happens next.' Keep trying. "Why did you grab me?"

"So you could finish the story. I've finished all your old stuff, and I've read as far as you've written down on this one, and I want to know what happens next."

"You mean that every time one of my old manuscripts disappeared, that it was you reading it?"

"Yes, but I've finished them. What happens next?"

"And when you took paper, and typewriter ribbons, and pens..."

"I was trying to make stories. But I can't! I'm only a time warp, and I can't create! Even with all the same materials, *you* can create stories, and all I can do is make a mess! If I try really hard, I can return stuff I took near where I got it from, but usually it comes out at random. I need you to make the stories."

"So you grabbed me." An awful thought swept through me. "Can you put me back?"

"But I want a story!" Definitely the wail of a small frustrated child.

"I can't write in the middle of a time warp."

"But you said that a writer, by definition, was a person who couldn't stop writing."

Just what I needed: a small child (I'm using the term loosely) with a retentive memory, among its *other* retentive qualities, who'd apparently been auditing my writing classes. "There are some things that will stop a writer. No paper, no pencils, no light, no time. I need my desk and my writing supplies, but even more, I need my family, my world, my life, and my experience. I need time, flowing past me in an orderly fashion, giving me structure to hang events on. I need time for these events to stir around in my subconscious, before they come out again as ideas and stories. I can't write in a time warp."

"But I want the story! I have to know what happens next!"

"Then you'll have to let me go. Once I get back home, I can continue to write, and then you'll have the rest of the story—but you had better give it back pretty soon; my editor wants it too."

"You can give him a copy."

"Only if you don't grab it before I have a chance to copy it. I'll make a deal with you. I'll make an extra copy of everything I write, and I'll put it in the bottom drawer of my desk, and you can take it from there. In return, I want you to stop grabbing everything else."

"You'll give me a copy of *all* your stories?"

"All of them." A higher copying bill is a small price to pay for not being dragged out of bed in the middle of the night like this.

"Okay. But you've got to keep giving me stories. If you stop, I'll grab you again, and hold onto you until I *do* figure out how to tap your subconscious. And I want the rest of this story right away. I really want to know what happens next."

My typewriter slipped away from under my fingers and the gray murk swung around me and turned black. The next thing I knew it was morning, and my daughter was standing over my bed, yelling at me because her alarm hadn't gone off and I hadn't wakened her and now she was going to be late for school unless I got up right that second and drove her to school. And the clock was still flashing.

So I got up and drove her to school, and I came home and reset the clock, and I went to the typewriter and finished the story. And now I'm hard at work on another one. Most writers' deadlines are set by human editors, but mine are set by the time warp.

GOLDEN VANITY

Edward lay sprawled face down in the mud, listening to the ringing of his ears. Above his head he could dimly hear the herald proclaiming his opponent, Sir Orland the Invincible, victor of this round in the Autumn Tourney of the Society for the Re-Creation of the Age of Chivalry. Sir Orland strode off the field to get ready for the next round, and the herald bent concernedly over Edward.

"Are you injured, my lord? Shall I summon the chirurgeon?"

Edward rolled over, tried to sit up and protest that he didn't need a doctor, and blacked out.

The next thing he knew he was lying on a cot, stripped of his armor, being sponged with cool water. It was very quiet in the chirurgeon's tent, enabling him to hear every word of the heated argument going on just outside.

"You could have killed him!" The voice was that of his twin sister, Ellen; Lady Eleanor the Perfect, who never did anything wrong, who never raised her voice or lost her calm dignity, while Edward bounced from scrape to crisis. He'd never heard her so upset.

"Lady Eleanor," Sir Orland sounded tired and annoyed. "If your brother would play by the rules of the lists and acknowledge the blows he receives, he would not have to be beaten senseless. Talk to him, not to me! And I warn you, if he pulls this stunt again, I am going to call your parents and suggest that they refuse to sign the fighter's waiver for him. Perhaps by the time he's old enough to sign it for himself, he'll have learned more sense."

"That wouldn't do the slightest bit of good," Ellen said bitterly. "They heartily approve of his getting beaten up—they think it will make him grow up to be a proper man."

Sir Orland whistled. "Like that, is it? Perhaps he ought to give up fighting altogether—sounds like he gets plenty of it at home."

"He wants to be a knight."

"Trying to prove something to his parents? Well, it's none of my business. However, my lady, I strongly suggest that you persuade him to alter his fighting style. Remember that he is allegedly fighting for *your* honor." Footsteps sloshed off through the mud, and Edward heard Ellen sigh as she entered the tent.

"Edward, are you all right?"

Edward stared miserably at the ceiling, and Ellen turned anxiously to the chirurgeon.

"He'll be fine, my lady." The chirurgeon got up to pour Edward a cup of Gatorade. Edward took a cautious sip. It tasted wonderful, which meant that he needed it badly—normally the stuff was quite unpalatable. "It was more the heat than anything else."

"In the future, my lord," the chirurgeon continued severely, "I would strongly suggest that you take off your armor between fights, drink lots of water, and take salt tablets when you need them. It is *not* heroic to collapse from the heat. For now, just go home, stay out of the sun, and take it easy for the rest of the day. You should be back to normal in the morning."

"Okay." Edward shoved aside the mug of Gatorade—it was beginning to taste terrible. He swung his legs over the side of the cot, resolutely ignoring the slightly shaky feeling moving gave him.

Eleanor picked up Edward's tunic and passed it to him. "I'll go start packing our gear, my lord. Join me when you're ready." She gathered up an armful of armor, nodded her thanks to the chirurgeon, and left the tent.

"That's quite a lady," the chirurgeon remarked.

"My sister," Edward said curtly. He was feeling terrible enough without more people praising Ellen. He was even more of a klutz in comparison with Ellen, and people had been comparing them since they were born.

Perhaps the chirurgeon sensed some of what he was feeling, or maybe he had a sister too, for he simply reminded Edward to drink lots of liquids—non-alcoholic—and let him go.

Edward wandered miserably back to his pavilion. Ellen had packed everything except the tent itself, and several gallant young men were carrying the last chest to the car. Ellen looked relieved to see him and signaled him to take his place for taking the tent down.

As the tent smoothly collapsed between them, Edward saw something gleaming in the mud at his feet. Picking it up, he discovered it was some sort of arm ring, heavy enough to be real gold. He realized that he should turn it in to the Marshal, but he felt rather drawn to it. Looking towards the lists, he saw Sir Orland watching him from the other side of the field. "To Hell with the whole pack of supercilious bastards!" Edward shoved the arm ring in his belt pouch and turned away to help Ellen fold the tent together. He glanced back as they loaded the tent in the car, and he thought he saw Sir Orland smile. Well, Sir Orland wouldn't gloat over him next time they met! He'd show them all.

Fortunately their parents were out at some party or other when he and Ellen arrived home—not that his bruises ever required too much explanation, but he wasn't in the mood to make any. He holed up in his room to lick his wounds in private, and Ellen tactfully left him alone.

By the next morning he was feeling human enough to take some interest in life again, and the first thing he did was to pull the arm ring out of his pouch and study it. It actually did appear to be real gold. It was in the form of a coiled dragon, a most beautiful and elaborate piece of work. It must be incredibly valuable, but what was it doing lying in the mud? If it belonged to anyone in the Society, Edward would surely have seen it before; no one could own something like this and not show it off all over Court. Edward had the totally irrational feeling that it had somehow come there to look for him, that it was meant to be his.

He looked around his room for a safe hiding place for the arm ring, but quickly realized that there was no place safe enough to hide *this* from his parents, who tended to be first class snoops at unpredictable intervals. Just then Ellen tapped on his door on her way down to breakfast, so he hastily shoved it on his left arm, where it fit midway between elbow and shoulder as if it had been made for him, pulled his school uniform shirt and blazer over it, and headed for the breakfast room.

Over the next few days Edward became quite attached to the arm ring. He wore it constantly, but showed it to no one. It was his secret, even from Ellen; something that was his alone. He made up stories about it, how it had belonged to a great hero and how it traveled throughout the world seeking out new heroes, giving its wearer the strength of ten men and enabling him to outfight anyone—especially Sir Orland. And it had chosen Edward as its new hero, because it knew that he wasn't really the klutz everybody thought he was; it knew he was special and capable of heroic deeds of chivalry.

It was, therefore, quite a nasty shock when he discovered that the arm ring actually *was* enchanted.

It started at the next fighter practice, where Edward was being his usual stoic self. His opponent got in past Edward's guard, striking his left shoulder a numbing blow with the rattan "sword." "That doesn't really count as a blow," Edward thought. "I barely felt it." But the arm ring suddenly tightened savagely on his arm, forcing a cry of pain from him as his shield clattered to the ground, falling from an arm he couldn't use.

The pain let up almost immediately, and he quickly retrieved his shield and kept on fighting, but the arm ring kept tightening on him all evening, each time Edward failed to acknowledge a blow fast enough to suit it. By the end of the evening it had become a race to see if he could acknowledge the blows he received before the arm ring crippled him.

He went home after practice with a very sore arm, and tried to remove the arm ring. It wouldn't come off—in fact, it wouldn't budge. He tried soaking in the hottest water he could stand in the hopes that the metal would expand and loosen, but all he got was red skin and a warm, firmly-stuck arm ring. He borrowed a hacksaw from his father's workbench and tried to cut it off. It didn't even scratch, but his arm certainly did. He wound up with a bloody, firmly-stuck arm ring, as well as blood all over the counter and sink. Blinking back tears of frustration and pain, he opened the door and yelled. "Ellen!"

The sound of a recorder being played in the next room suddenly ceased and Ellen appeared in the hall, recorder in hand. "I'm sorry, was I making a racket?" Her eyes widened as she took in the blood running down his arm. "Careful, don't drip on the carpet or you'll have to explain it to Mother." She pitched her recorder in the general direction of her bed and hastily joined him in the bathroom.

"What happened? If you're trying to kill yourself, I believe that it's your wrists you're supposed to cut."

"Very funny." Actually Edward felt a little better. Ellen's fabled perfection could be trying, but she was great to have around in a real crisis. "I was trying to get this arm ring off."

"Did you try cold cream?"

"No, but I did try soap and hot water, and they didn't work. And it's very odd that the hacksaw won't cut it; gold is supposed to be a soft metal."

"Are you sure that the hacksaw was hitting it at all? It looks like all it cut was you."

"All right, *you* try it."

Ellen took the hacksaw, rinsed the blood off it, and very carefully sawed at the arm ring. She couldn't so much as scratch it either, but at least she managed to miss Edward's arm.

"You're right", she said, giving up. "There is definitely something very strange about that thing. Why were you trying to take it off—and where did it come from in the first place?"

While Ellen got out the first aid kit, patched up his arm, and washed the blood off the counter, Edward gave her a reasonably accurate account of how the arm ring had come to be in his possession and the effect it was having on his actions. "I'd gladly turn it in to the Marshal now—if I could just get the damn thing off! It's ruining my fighting!"

"If it's enchanted, which it certainly appears to be, it probably wouldn't let you turn it in anyway. Presumably it has a purpose and you're stuck with it—or in it—until that purpose is accomplished. Maybe it's supposed to teach you a different way to fight." She paused to consider the matter. "You're a bit on the small side—"

"So are you!" Edward hated being told he was small, and Ellen ought to know that by now.

"Since I don't fight, it's no disadvantage for me. But it shouldn't be impossible to work around—after all, not all the knights in the Middle Ages were giants; there must be fighting techniques that work for smaller men. Or maybe you're supposed to make up for what you lack in brawn with brains. Do some research on the problem." She yawned. "I'm going to bed. Call me if you need help with your jacket in the morning."

She left, and Edward dug out the Society fighter's handbook and started reading.

He spent the next week, while his arm healed, reading everything he could find about medieval chivalry, honor, and fighting. By the time he arrived at the next tourney he wasn't entirely sure what century he was in.

He was very careful in his first few fights, parrying for all he was worth, avoiding as many blows as possible and quickly acknowledging any that hit him. To his surprise, he actually won his first few rounds, and wound up matched against Sir Orland for the fifth round.

The lists were the usual sea of mud. It seemed to be a basic rule of nature that it always rained before a tourney and then the sun came out and broiled the fighters, enabling them to slip in the mud while getting sunstroke. Today, however, Edward's luck seemed to be in; it was Sir Orland who slid and fell flat on his back, with his helmet slipping to leave him temporarily blinded.

It was the perfect opening; all Edward had to do was take one step forward and hold his sword to Sir Orland's throat and he would be the victor. And if he defeated one of the Society's best knights in combat, they would almost be forced to knight him. And that would show everyone who looked down at him—

That would show everyone who looked down at him that he'd do anything and take advantage of anything for a title he hadn't really earned. That would show everyone who looked down on him that they were right to despise him. *There's no honor in defeating someone who can't see to defend himself,* Edward thought. *If I win like this, they should knight the mud!* He lowered his sword and stepped back to allow Sir Orland to pick himself up and adjust his helmet.

Once Sir Orland was back on his feet and battle was joined again, Edward was too busy to think of anything but avoiding serious injury while Sir Orland mopped up the field with him. At the end of the fight, when Sir Orland announced his intention of knighting him on the field "for valiant and chivalrous conduct," Edward was so surprised that he nearly fell over as he knelt. As Sir Orland's sword touched his shoulder, Edward felt the arm ring grow warm. Looking to see what it was going to do now, he was astonished to find it slipping down his arm, over his hand, and back into the mud. He reached for it, but was stopped by Sir Orland's hand assisting him to rise from his knees.

"Let it go," Sir Orland said softly. "You don't need it anymore."

CONNECTICAT
Elisabeth Waters & Raul S. Reyes

It had been a difficult death. The illness contracted in the humid lowlands had been bad enough. But the young man's dissolute life had left its mark on his character as well, and as he died the Lama found it hard to keep the parts of his being together. Each one threatened to leave separately as the corresponding sense died in the body. It took all of the lama's patient counsel to keep the young man's consciousness together.

Finally the consciousness was free of the body, but the Lama remained, coaching the young man's spirit as it traversed through that dark realm on the other side of death. It was too much to hope that he might be reborn as a healthy son of a wealthy family, or even as a younger son dedicated by his family to a wealthy lamasery, with sufficient endowment to pursue a life of contemplation. But at least he might be kept from the life of a poor beggar, a criminal, or, worse yet, an animal.

There were demons on the path. The Lama explained these were illusions. So also were the clear streams and soft, grassy resting places by the path. The young man's spirit must pass all of these on his path to rebirth.

More serious were the distractions of the flesh. The young man had been all too prone to them in life, and the plump young maidens beckoning to him from cushioned grottos, pots of beer and wine by their sides, were almost too much for his shade. The Lama explained that they were traps for the unwary soul and the grottos were undesirable wombs. So far the disembodied spirit had listened to his teaching and passed those illusions.

The path to rebirth was difficult and the spirit was tiring rapidly. The Lama intoned a chant to give him strength. It flowed to the young man's spirit and revived his energy. The Lama allowed himself a moment of rest; the chant had taken some of his strength. Too late he realized his mistake.

The young man's soul, revitalized by the chant, became aware of a bower under some rhododendrons. A saucy young girl with sleek dark hair and sly cat eyes beckoned to him from a pile of cushioned rugs. A jar of sweet wine waited next to her. The Lama shouted a warning, but it was too late. The young man sank to her side and was lost.

Christina sat in her car at the New Canaan train station, waiting for the train from New York and her mother's dinner guest. In the passenger seat Tashi, her Burmese tomcat, protested vociferously the delay in their return home and his release from his carrier. Christina was just as disgusted with the situation, but not quite as vocal.

"It isn't my fault, Tashi," she protested. "I made the appointment with the vet three months ago, and I certainly had no way of knowing that mother would pick tonight to invite some Tibetan Lama she met in New York out here for dinner—or that his arrival would be timed so that we'd have to come here straight from the vet."

Tashi was definitely unimpressed by this argument. His suggestion, however, was not helpful.

"I can't tell my mother where to go; after all, my parents *do* live next door to us." She twisted to meet the cat's eyes. He stared back. "And while I'm sure that respect for one's parents is a totally foreign concept to you, it does mean something to me—even if my respect doesn't extend to marrying and providing them with grandchildren right now." She sighed. "I wish I weren't an only child; if I had brothers or sisters, *they* could provide grandchildren. I'm perfectly happy living with you, and I don't need some man cluttering up my house and my life!"

Both of them suddenly cocked their heads to listen to the sound of the warning bells at the railroad crossing two blocks before the station. "Oh, good," Christina said. "At least the train's on time. I'll be back in a couple of minutes—at this time of day there won't be many people." The next train, she knew, would be a multi-car express straight from Grand Central Station, instead of the two-car "turkey killer" that connected with the main line at Stamford during non-commute hours. If she were meeting *that* train, she'd be lucky to get her car into the parking lot.

Finding her mother's guest was easy, even though he was dressed in a conventional suit rather than whatever type of robe a Lama traditionally wore. Only five people got off the train, three of them were women, and the other man was black. Besides, he was the only one with a shaved head.

Christina was opening her mouth to greet the man when he forestalled her.

"You must be Miss Lang," he said, smiling and extending his hand. "Your mother said you'd be meeting me."

"Yes, I am," Christina replied, shaking hands with him. His handshake was warm and firm, and felt oddly as if some sort of electrical current ran through his body. "I hope you don't mind cats," she said nervously. "Tashi and I are on the way home from the vet. He's in a carrier, so he won't shed on your clothes, but he's not a happy cat at the moment."

"Tashi?" the Lama raised his eyebrows. "That's an unusual name for a cat. Why was he named that?"

Christina shrugged, "I don't know. The breeder called him something different, but when I bought him—well, it just seemed like that should be his name. Why? Does it mean something in Tibetan?"

"There is a holy man called the Tashi Lama."

"Like the Dalai Lama?"

"More or less. The Tashi Lama outranks the Dalai Lama spiritually, but the Dalai Lama outranks him politically."

"Oh." Christina opened the passenger door of the car and reached for the carrier. "I'll put him in the back seat, so he'll be out of your way." She knew her mother would have a fit if she made a guest ride with the cat in his lap.

"That is not necessary," he replied. Before Christina realized his intent he had opened the carrier and cradled Tashi in one arm while he tossed the empty carrier in the back seat and slipped into the car. Christina closed the door quickly before Tashi decided to get out and explore downtown New Canaan, and went to get into the driver's seat.

She half-expected Tashi to have made a good start on the job of clawing the Lama to ribbons, but to her amazement the two of them sat there staring into each others' eyes as if they were communicating.

She fastened her seat belt, looked to be sure that her passenger had fastened his, started the engine, and pulled out of the parking lot. She drove in silence for several minutes before saying, "We'll stop at my house to drop off Tashi, if that's all right with you. My parents' house is next door, but if we go to my house first, we can get the cat hair off your suit."

"You share your life with a cat, and you worry about a little cat hair?" the Lama asked in amusement.

"Not usually," Christina replied. "Most of my sweaters match Tashi's fur, so I usually pass a casual inspection." She sighed. "Unfortunately, at least as far as my appearance is concerned, my mother's inspections are far from casual." She smiled reassuringly at him. "But you're probably safe enough; you're a guest."

He chuckled briefly, continuing to stroke Tashi, who sat quietly in his arms. "How old is Tashi?" he inquired.

"Three years old next month," Christina replied.

The Lama nodded slowly, apparently pleased with her answer for some unknown reason of his own. Christina gave a mental shrug and concentrated her attention on the sharp curves of the road.

To Christina's horror, her spinster status became a topic of discussion at the dinner table. In addition to Christina, her parents and the Lama, there were two other couples who were friends of the Langs. Since they came to Mrs. Lang's parties frequently, Christina thought they must surely be tired of hearing her mother bemoan her daughter's unwed state. But no one Mrs. Lang invited to her house would ever be rude enough to say so. Either that, or after a few of the drinks her father served before dinner and the wine with dinner, they didn't notice that they had heard this conversation many times before.

Mrs. Lang began with semi-polite inquiries into the family of her guest, who turned out to be the type of Lama forbidden to marry and thus had family consisting of his parents (father deceased), his brother (another celibate Lama), and his sister (married, four children).

"At least your mother has the consolation of grandchildren," she murmured. "Her father and I do so hope that Christina will find a nice young man and settle down soon." She looked at her daughter and sighed. "She could be such a pretty girl if she'd just make a bit of an effort."

"You mean spend an hour each morning on make-up, an afternoon a week at the hairdresser's, and one day each month buying new clothes," Christina said lightly. "I know that I could look prettier than I do, but I have no reason to put in that kind of time and energy. My clothes are decent and appropriate, and since I spend most of my time in a library with my nose in a book, make-up would be a complete waste of time. Besides, it makes my skin break out."

"But you'll never get a husband that way!" her mother protested. She turned to the Lama. "Do you have this problem in your country?"

He shook his head. "Not in the manner that you do. My sister married the man my parents chose for her; there a girl is expected to obey her parents."

Christina decided to change the subject before he could suggest that her parents choose a husband for her. "What do you think of my mother's garden?" she asked, indicating the variety of plants surrounding the terrace where they were eating. "Do you have any of the same plants in Tibet?"

"We have rhododendrons," he replied. "I was admiring them earlier, Mrs. Lang; they are truly beautiful."

Mrs. Lang smiled complacently. "Yes, they do quite nicely here—although I did have a bit of trouble when Christina first got that cat of hers."

"Really?" the Lama sounded fascinated.

"It was dreadful," Mrs. Lang assured him. "Every time he got out—which fortunately wasn't too often; Christina is a conscientious girl and is generally meticulous about keeping him indoors—he would come over here and burrow in under the rhododendrons. It wasn't good for them at all."

"It's Tashi's favorite flower," Christina explained. "Finally we got a bush for my yard and Father extended the fence around my patio to enclose it, so now Tashi has his very own rhododendron and doesn't bother Mother's."

"A sensible solution," the Lama remarked, and the subject of conversation changed to landscaping.

Alone in his hotel room later that night, the Lama prepared for bed, turned out the lights, sat comfortably on the floor in lotus position, and cast his mind towards his brother's monastery in Tibet. The contact came quickly.

"Have you found him yet, brother?" the Tashi Lama inquired.

"Yes, elder brother, I have found our erring nephew. It was as you said: once I arrived in New York I was led to him."

"I sensed that he was there. Is he one of their 'street people'? Surely he would be rather young for that, unless he was born to—tell me he was not reborn in the womb of a drug addict."

19

"No, it is not that bad. He is in excellent physical condition. But still, this may prove more difficult than we had anticipated."

"Brother, all I asked was that you find him and instruct him, so that he may improve his way of life, and, if possible, that you bring him home. What is the difficulty?"

"Perhaps I should tell you how I found him. As we arranged, I gave a talk at the Open Center, which was reasonably well attended. One of the ladies in the audience, a Mrs. Lang, came up to me afterwards and invited me to her home in Connecticut for dinner the following night. I felt that I should accept her invitation, and so I did, taking the train to New Canaan the next afternoon. Mrs. Lang's daughter Christina picked me up at the station. She was on her way home from the vet with her cat: a Burmese male called Tashi."

Several seconds of silence preceded the Tashi Lama's reply. "You are quite sure that it is not merely a coincidence of names?"

"I held him, and I looked into his eyes. He will be three years old next month, and he has such a passion for rhododendrons that they have planted him his very own plant, so that he will leave Mrs. Lang's alone. I have no doubt that he is our nephew."

"A cat." The Tashi Lama sighed. "Well, that does make the job harder, but it can still be done. Will the girl give him to you? Then you could bring him home, and we could do the transformation here."

"I have not asked her to give me her cat, nor do I feel it would be right so to do. I believe that he owes a debt, either to her or to her parents."

"What sort of debt?"

"A debt of family. Christina is twenty-five, an only child, unmarried, and so bound to Tashi that she refuses to look elsewhere for companionship or love."

"And, like our sister, I suppose her parents want grandchildren."

"They do; they devoted half of the dinner hour to the subject. As for our sister, I imagine she has quite a few grandchildren by now. I gather that Tashi does quite well in stud fees."

"Stud fees?" The Tashi Lama considered the implications of that statement and made his decision. "I refuse to tell our sister that she has grandchildren who are cats."

"I do not think the knowledge would gladden her heart."

"Would this Christina marry him and bear children if he were to be transformed? And would she make him a proper wife?"

"I believe that she would—and I fear she would be a better wife than he a husband. I intend to see her tomorrow, and I shall sound her out on the subject."

"Keep me informed of your progress. Advise me when you are ready to do the transformation. Rest well, younger brother."

"May your path be bright this day, elder brother."

The Lama opened his eyes, rose smoothly from the floor, and went to bed.

He awoke around nine the next morning, ate breakfast, and then made his way to the New York Public Library. It was not difficult to find Christina. She was in the genealogy section, going through the index of death records for the various boroughs of New York City. He sat down opposite her at the long table, his talent for stillness rendering him invisible to her, the other patrons, and the library staff. He spent several hours observing her while she did her research.

He had been correct to suspect that she had passion and determination; here, in the work she did, it was visible. To his eyes she glowed slightly every time she found something she had been searching for, another link in the chain she was tracing. She worked continuously for hours, apparently oblivious to such bodily concerns as lunch. When she finally gathered her notes together and returned the books she had been using, it was late afternoon.

He followed her as she left the library, coming up to her just as she walked out the front door. "Good afternoon, Miss Lang."

Christina started. "Oh, good afternoon, Gomchen." She had been told yesterday that 'Gomchen' was the proper form of address, although it was a title, not a name. Apparently Tibetans did not uses names socially. "I didn't see you; were you in the library?"

"Yes. I saw you there. Did you have a profitable day?"

"Very much so. I've found five new people on this branch of the family." She laughed. "Some days I can't seem to find anything and I'd swear that some of my ancestors were the products of spontaneous generation."

He chuckled at the joke, then said, "It seems strange to me that you spend so much effort tracing a lineage that ends with you. Do you not wish to marry and have children to extend the line forward?"

Christina looked sad. "Yes, actually I do. I like children, and I wish I had some of my own. But for that, you need a husband—and, as the saying goes, 'the more I see of men, the more I like my cat.' It's too bad I can't marry him."

"Actually, that can be arranged."

Christina stared at him. "I was joking."

"Your marriage would make your parents very happy," he said persuasively.

"They certainly talked about it enough at dinner last night, didn't they? But I don't think they're so desperate that they would welcome a cat as a son-in-law."

"But if Tashi were human..."

"Tashi is not human."

"He can be."

She looked at him out of the corner of her eyes. "You're not used to the heat here—or maybe the pollution is getting to you."

"The heat does not bother me," he said calmly, "but a drink would be pleasant. My hotel puts on an excellent tea this time of day. Please do me the honor of joining me."

Christina considered running for Grand Central, but it was much too hot. Besides what could happen to her in a hotel dining room?

She was never sure afterwards how he had managed it, but by the time Namtso Gomchen escorted her to the station, several hours later, she had agreed to marry her cat, as soon as he could be transformed to human. "After all," she pointed out, "we will need blood tests for the marriage license, and the clerk at the Town Hall is bound to notice if one of them comes from a vet."

Namtso Gomchen took the train to New Canaan Saturday morning to perform the transformation. As before, Christina drove him home from the station. He exited from the car in one fluid movement, his eyes scanning the woods behind her house with delight. It was so lush and verdant, so unlike his homeland. His briefcase, containing his monk's robe, and a few other items he had not described to Christina, was in his right fist. He closed the car door behind him and waited for her to lead him in.

Tashi came out to meet them, or rather her. For some reason he affected to ignore Gomchen Namtso. The learned Lama returned the compliment.

"Is there somewhere I can change?" he asked. He had learned that Westerners had unusual ideas about clothing. It was considered appropriate for a young lady to appear in public in less cloth than it took to make a scarf if she was bathing at the beach, but if he disrobed within her home it was a serious breach of etiquette unless he did so in a room set aside for that purpose. She tilted her head toward a door.

"The bathroom is over there," she replied. He nodded his thanks and entered it. In a few moments he reappeared, clad in a brilliant saffron robe, barefoot, with a rosary-necklace around his neck. The "beads" were made of bone disks. Christina recalled what little she had heard of Tibet and decided against asking what the bone had come from.

"Will you brew me some tea?" he asked, handing her a small package of the black Chinese tea he preferred. "I will need it for the ceremony." She nodded and went into the kitchen. Strictly speaking, it was not part of the ritual, but he needed some fortification prior to the ceremony. While she was busy he scooped Tashi up in one motion that caught the feline by surprise and cradled it in the crook of his arm.

"Well, my unrepentant nephew," he whispered in Tibetan. "I hope you have enjoyed your life of cream and 'Meow Mix'." The brand name came out oddly in the stream of Tibetan. "But now you must return to your proper life, and your proper duties. It should not be too onerous. She is attractive, has a good home, and her family is wealthy. Your main duties will be on the pillows, to provide her family with heirs. 'Right up your alley'." It sounded odd in Tibetan.

The cheerful whistle of the teapot called him to the kitchen and he took Tashi in with him, his briefcase in his other hand. Christina smiled at him in greeting. He smiled back, making sure the door had swung shut before releasing Tashi. "Thank you," he said. "Tea is good in the morning. Would you like some of this?" he asked.

She smiled and shook her head. "I'll stick to Earl Gray," she replied.

He shrugged and added salt to his cup, then took a small jar out of his briefcase. Salt was readily available, but yaks, and yak butter, were scarce in New York and Connecticut. Christina kept her eyes on her own cup, and pretended not to notice that he was stirring butter into his tea.

"What do you need me to do for the ritual?" she asked.

"Just leave the room and wait outside. I must concentrate so that my brother may come here."

"The Tashi Lama will come here?" she asked.

He nodded.

Christina tried to think of an intelligent reply to this. Unable to come up with one, she took another sip of her tea, then stared down into the cup. When she looked up.

Namtso Gomchen was setting up a pair of beaten brass lamps, filled with yak butter, on the counter top.

"We must move the table and chairs out of the room," he said. She set about to help him, glad of something to do. In moments the kitchen was stripped of all movable furniture, leaving a fair expanse of ceramic tile floor. He set the lamps on the tiles and settled down before them, placing a strangely docile Tashi between them. "Thank you," he said. "That will be all." It was a dismissal.

Outside she sat in a chair and twisted her cup between her hands, staring down into it, as if she could divine the future in the swirling liquid. The scent of the butter lamps, mixed with incense, wafted under the door, along with the sound of clapping and low, sonorous chanting. Twice there were sharp explosive words that made her hair stand on end. Suddenly she remembered something.

"The smoke detector!" she gasped. She set the tea aside and raced into the kitchen. It had not yet gotten high enough to set off the alarm, but the lamps cast a lurid glow over a smoky, scented cloud.

Christina reached for the switch which would disable the smoke detector, but the sight of Namtso Gomchen stopped her in mid-motion. He was stiff in the lotus position, pale, and hardly breathing. Tashi sat immobile before him, staring up at his face. Slowly, a sigh escaped the Lama's lips, longer than any sigh had a right to be, and suddenly the Lama began to straighten up.

With a shock Christina realized he was growing. In moments he sat a full two inches taller, his shoulders were wider, and his hands were no longer the soft hands of a monk, but long and strong. Namtso Gomchen was no longer in her kitchen. In his place was a tall, lean, strongly built man, his skin tight over his skull, his face long and hard-featured, with eyes as black and hard as obsidian.

So this is what he meant when he said that the Tashi Lama would come here, Christina thought. Stunned, she sank slowly to the floor, her breath coming back in painful gulps.

The Lama did not seem to notice her presence. He continued to chant, only this time his voice was wild and haunted, and the language no longer sounded Tibetan. She recalled stories Namtso Gomchen had told at the dinner party. Stories of the Bon, the original people of Tibet, whose blood ran in the Khampa, the warrior/brigands of later Tibet, and of their religion, also called Bon. Tales of black magic and sorcery, not eradicated by Buddhism, but incorporated into the Tibetan version. She sat very still, not daring to move or speak.

Suddenly the Lama clapped his hands, the sound a thunderbolt in her head, and kept his hands together for a long time. Slowly he spread them apart, and fire grew between them, elongated, and reached out to Tashi, bathing him in flames.

Christina gasped and pressed a fist to her mouth. Tashi writhed in agony, and began to grow, change in outline, and shed hair. A distant part of her mind noted that he shed hair constantly anyway. A long moan of pain escaped from between his lips as he became more man-like, and he fell on his side, his face, a human face, contorted with the pain of his transformation.

Another handclap to split her head with the sound of it, and the fire vanished. The Lama sagged forward in exhaustion, shrinking back into the form and appearance of Namtso Gomchen. Christina found herself breathing again, propped against the wall, and became aware of two distinct sounds: the smoke alarm, and the telephone.

She dragged herself to her feet, hit the switch to silence the smoke alarm, then picked up the phone. "Hello?" she said. "Yes, Daddy, that was my smoke alarm... No, everything's okay, you don't have to come over... No, I'm fine, really. I was just cleaning the oven and it had a bit more grease than I realized. It's under control... No, I haven't forgotten about dinner; I'll be over at six-thirty tonight. Goodbye, Daddy."

She turned to the Lama. "You won't need the oven for anything for the next few hours, will you?"

He looked surprised at the odd question. "No. Why?"

"Good." Christina set the oven dials to self-clean, engaged the locking mechanism, and started the cycle. "Daddy isn't dashing over here right now, but I bet he'll drop in some time this afternoon, and I'd better have a just-cleaned oven." She sighed. "I try not to lie to my parents; it makes life much easier when all I have to remember is the truth."

She looked at Tashi and added, "And when the truth won't serve, we'd better have a very convincing story." She went to sit next to him. He was still lying on his side, motionless and silent. She pillowed his head in her lap, put out a hand and gently stroked his hair, which was dark, short and curly. "Tashi, are you all right?"

Tashi gave her a pained glance and closed his eyes.

She turned to Namtso Gomchen in alarm. "What's wrong? Can't he talk?"

"He can talk," the Lama replied calmly. "The transformation is a bit of a shock, however, and it may take him a while to adjust."

Christina looked stricken. "What if he doesn't want to go through with this?"

"He has gone through this," Namtso Gomchen pointed out. "He is human again now."

Christina swallowed. "But what if he doesn't want to marry me?" Tashi's head twisted to butt up against her hand, as he always had when he wanted her to pet him. Automatically her hand stroked his hair.

"I do," he said. His voice was a soft purr. "I want to marry you and have children with you."

Christina blushed, and then suddenly realized what her mother would consider an appropriate wedding ceremony. Staging the opera "Aida," triumphal procession and all, would be simpler, quicker, and require fewer people. "I think we had better elope," she said firmly. "First we get married, then we tell my parents. They'll throw a gigantic party; but if we're already married, they can't insist on a big fancy wedding."

Tashi looked curious. "What are your wedding customs like?"

Christina shuddered, imagining her mother's version of same. "You don't want to know."

"But surely you do not intend to marry without your parents present!" It was the first time Christina had seen the Lama look shocked.

"If we get married in my church," she pointed out, "they read out the banns—it's a sort of announcement—for at least three weeks beforehand. And the church requires that the bride and groom have pre-marital counseling with a priest, who will, at the very least, ask us how we met, why we want to get married, and all sorts of questions about our future plans—to say nothing of our current religious beliefs and what we intend to teach our children. He's also bound to ask where Tashi lives, what he does for a living, and what his home parish is."

"I see your point," the Lama said.

"And we need another name for him," Christina went on. "I can't very well say that my husband is named after my cat—particularly when I can't produce the cat."

"He can take your surname when you marry," Namtso Gomchen said, "as a compliment to your family." He smiled suddenly. "As for a first name, it seems to me that 'Tom' would be appropriate."

"Thomas Lang." Christina nodded. "Sounds all right to me—is it okay with you, Tashi?"

He smiled up at her. "Just call me Tom."

The Lama stood up briskly and picked up his briefcase. "Very well, Tom. I brought clothing for you. You will accompany me back to the city."

Christina and Tashi started to protest together, but the Lama overruled them. "You do not want Mr. Lang to find you here before the wedding. Christina, come to my hotel

Monday morning. I shall arrange to have the blood tests done and find someone to marry the two of you as soon as possible." He pulled his nephew to his feet and headed for the bathroom. "Do not worry, Christina; you will not have to be alone for long."

It was less than a week, but Christina had never realized how lonely she could feel. By the next Friday, she was so glad to have Tashi home again that introducing him to her parents and telling them that she had eloped seemed a small price to pay.

Of course, the first question her mother asked was "Are you pregnant?"

"Not yet," Christina replied serenely, "but we plan to have children very soon." She realized that she had a death-grip on Tashi's hand and tried to loosen it a bit, but he simply squeezed her hand and smiled at her.

"And what do you do, Tom?" Mr. Lang asked.

This was one of the first questions covered in Tashi's coaching ('fifty all-purpose questions for cocktail parties' was how Christina had described it). "I am a student of philosophy, sir. And I believe that you are acquainted with my uncle, Namtso Gomchen."

By the end of the evening the Langs were enthusiastic about their new son-in-law, and Mrs. Lang was happily planning parties to introduce him to everyone she knew. Christina suspected that she was starting to plan a baby shower as well.

Two months, one gigantic wedding reception, and twenty-three dinner parties later, Christina woke up one morning feeling truly dreadful. Tashi was draped all over her as usual. *In some ways*, Christina thought, *I don't think he's ever going to get over being a cat. And now he takes up even more of the bed.* She started to sit up, but lay back down quickly—moving made her feel sick to her stomach.

Tashi had half-wakened when she moved, and now he absent-mindedly began to nuzzle her breast. Christina yelped and pushed him violently away. "Don't do that! It hurts!"

Tashi, who had not been expecting the shove, fell out of bed and landed hard on the floor. He sat up, groaning. "When I was a cat, I would have landed on my feet if you had done that," he complained. He looked at her. "What's wrong with you? You look as sick as I feel. What does your father put in those drinks he serves anyway?"

"About three ounces of alcohol per drink," Christina replied matter-of-factly. "How many did you have last night?"

"I can't count that high. Remember, I am only a simple cat."

"Tashi, that's not funny. Besides, if you drank like that in cat form, you'd die of alcohol poisoning."

"If I were a cat, I wouldn't be putting that garbage in my body. If I were a cat, I wouldn't have to go to your parents' stupid parties."

"My mother's stupid parties," Christina corrected him. "My father hates them as much as you do—why do you think he makes the drinks so strong?"

She tried to move and felt sick again. "Hand me the phone, will you?"

She dialed, still lying flat on her back. "Mother, do you know any good cures for morning sickness? I think I'll throw up if I try to get out of bed."

"That's wonderful, dear!" Her mother was obviously thrilled. "How far along are you? When is the baby due?"

"Mother, I'm not even sure I'm pregnant yet. I just feel very sick. Is there anything that can be done about it?"

"Saltines," her mother said promptly. "Keep a pack of them next to your bed and eat a few before you try to move in the morning. Have Tom get you some now." Christina relayed the instruction and he nodded and headed for the kitchen. Her mother was still babbling on. "Be sure to go see

Dr. Shaw today, and let me know your due date as soon as you figure it out. Oh, this is going to be such fun!"

Maybe for you it is, Christina thought as she hung up the phone. *It doesn't feel too great to me right now.*

To her mother's delight, Christina was indeed pregnant. Namtso Gomchen, who stopped by every couple of months to check on his nephew's spiritual progress (or lack of same) was delighted as well. It was he who told Christina that she carried twins.

"They will be human, won't they?" Christina asked uncertainly.

"Yes, of course," the Lama replied. "Why shouldn't they be?"

Christina led the way to the den. Tashi was sprawled along the couch, staring intently at the television. The Lama watched fish swimming about on the screen for several minutes. "What program is this?" he inquired.

"It's a video made for cats," Christina replied a bit grimly. "The breeder I got Tashi from gave it to him last Christmas. He liked it then, and now—well, he spends hours watching it every day. Most of his waking hours, in fact." She took a deep breath and finished in a rush. "Uncle, I think the transformation is failing."

"What?"

"I think he's turning back into a cat. Maybe his humanity went to the babies—I don't know. But ever since I've been pregnant, he's been more and more cat-like. He refuses to go anywhere, even next door to my parent's parties. He lies around all day, napping and watching this video, but sometimes I wake up at night and hear him pacing about the house." She looked uneasily at the Lama. "I've tried to be a good wife to him, truly I have. I don't think I'm doing anything to cause this," she gestured at Tashi, who was still staring raptly at the screen and ignoring them, "but I just don't know! Uncle, what shall I do?"

Namtso Gomchen sighed. "It's not your fault. I told my brother at the start that I feared you would make a better wife than our nephew would a husband."

"He's still very nice, for a cat," Christina said earnestly. "But when he looks like a human, people expect more of him. My parents are having fits; mother is mortally offended that we're not coming to her parties—but he *won't* and I feel sick so much of the time..."

"I could take him back to Tibet with me," the Lama said, frowning at his nephew. "Perhaps in a monastery his concentration on higher thoughts would improve."

"How do we know he's not concentrating on higher thoughts now? He can do that as well as a cat in Connecticut as he can as a man in a monastery in Tibet," Christina pointed out. "And I don't want him to go back to Tibet. I love him; he's all I have left of Tashi!"

"You will have your children soon," Namtso Gomchen reminded her. "You won't be alone."

Tashi's head swung with preternatural suddenness to face them. He even gave the impression of twitching his ears. He jumped over the back of the couch and stalked gracefully across the room to stand beside Christina. "Don't badger her, uncle," he said firmly. "I am not going back to Tibet. I am staying with Christina."

"And the children?" his uncle challenged. "What kind of a father are you going to be?"

Tashi smiled sardonically. "As good as any other cat." He looked thoughtful for a moment, then continued, "I've been a cat, and I've been a human. It's better to be a cat; it's a much more contemplative existence. Humans alternate between rushing around making themselves too busy to think, and drinking themselves into a stupor so that they won't *have* to think.

He glared at the Lama in open challenge. "Keep me in a human body as long as you can, uncle, but you can't make me into that kind of human. No matter what form I wear, I *am* a cat."

"Do you expect Christina to raise your children alone?" the Lama protested.

"I'll be here," Tashi replied. "Unlike her father, who spent her entire childhood working in New York, and came home each night in such a bad mood that she used to hide from him."

"Is this true, Christina?" the Lama asked.

"Well, he didn't *mean* to be so cross all the time," Christina said hastily. "But you've done the commute, even if it's only been a few times and not during rush hour. Daddy would get up every morning, spend an hour on a crowded train, half-an-hour on an even more crowded subway, work a full day, then spend half-an-hour on the subway and another hour on the train. Then he'd get home and Mother would tell him everything that had gone wrong with *her* day, and..."

"And they'd have a couple of drinks apiece to calm down, and if Christina was lucky, they'd simply ignore her," Tashi finished the explanation. "If she wasn't lucky, they'd hit her. Cats make much better parents than that!"

Christina was still trying to defend her parents. "They didn't beat me or anything like that," she told the Lama, who was looking grave. "They never spanked me when I didn't know why they were doing it."

"Because you were there." Tashi did not sound as forgiving. "I've seen too damn much of your parents since we got married—and I hope you never plan to ask them to baby-sit."

Christina dropped into the nearest chair and burst into tears. "He's right," she sobbed to Namtso Gomchen, who was staring at his nephew in shock. "He *has* seen too much of my parents—he's picking up Daddy's vocabulary."

"Merciful Buddha!" The Lama looked from his weeping niece to his nephew, who had curled up on the arm of her chair and was patting her cheek with his fingertips.

"And my mother complains all the time that he's lazy— and I want my cat back!" Christina wailed.

Tashi faced his uncle squarely. "Perhaps it was not an accident that I was reborn as a cat, uncle. Change me back. Please."

"Christina?" the Lama asked.

Christina mopped her face with her sleeve. "Change him back. He's right. Cathood is a more contemplative existence. And he's a very good cat."

"And your parents?"

"We'll tell them he went back to Tibet with you for a visit, and in a month or two you can write and tell us of his untimely accidental death." Christina shrugged. "As long as no one questions her grandchildren's legitimacy, my mother will be happy. And as long as Mother's happy, Daddy's happy."

"How will you explain Tashi's reappearance as a cat?"

"Nobody knows he's been gone. In a few months I'll get a card from the vet, reminding me to bring him in for shots and then I'd have to explain his absence, but right now, as far as anyone knows, Tashi's been here all along." She faced the Lama. "He *has* been here all along. Please, change him back." She rested a hand on her abdomen. "I have my children; my parents will have their grandchildren. He's done what he agreed to do."

Namtso Gomchen sighed. "Very well." He picked up his briefcase. "Go set up the kitchen—and this time, please turn off the smoke detector before we start."

"Absolutely." Christina smiled radiantly.

The twins were born at St. Joseph's Hospital a few months (one baby shower, six dinner parties) later. Christina named them Christopher and Katherine, and called them Kit and Cat. Tashi seemed to approve.

ICE PRINCESS

It was very cold when Sharon woke up. At first she thought that the heater in her cottage had stopped working—this happened occasionally, and it got cold before dawn this high in the mountains. Then she realized that there was a lot more light in the room than there should have been, considering the fact that she was supposed to be at the rink by 5:55 a.m. and on the ice by 6:00. *I guess I shouldn't have stayed out so late last night*, she thought. *I must have slept through my alarm. Thank God I don't have a lesson on the first session.* She groaned.

"Dost thou always sleep until the sun is halfway up the sky?" The voice was that of a very young girl.

Sharon didn't have a roommate, and children under age 18 weren't allowed in the cottages. Her eyes snapped open. It didn't help much; even with extended-wear contact lenses it took a few minutes to get the world in focus in the morning. And when it was in focus, it wasn't *her* world.

She was still in her own bed, and her bed table was next to it, but everything else had changed. Her room was gone; the bed and table now stood in the middle of a large round room with grey stone walls. There were four large windows at intervals in the walls, and a strong crosswind blew across the room, making Sharon's eyes feel as if the lenses were drying out and sticking to them. Fortunately she kept a bottle of saline solution on the bed table. She put a couple of drops in each eye and blinked several times. Excess salt water dripped down her cheeks, but now she could see the little girl sitting on the foot of her bed.

The child seemed to be about ten years old, and she looked exactly like Sharon herself had looked at that age. She had nondescript pale grey eyes, long brown hair, parted neatly in the middle, with a thick braid hanging over each shoulder, and she wore a long white dress with silver edging around a square neckline and a white shawl around her shoulders. She was shivering in the wind, but she didn't seem to notice.

"Art thou crying?" she asked curiously. "A princess is not supposed to cry. Mother says so."

Sharon felt as though she had fallen down a rabbit hole. "Where is your mother?"

"Our mother," the child corrected her. "Thou art my sister, Sharon, dost thou not remember?"

"I'm an only child," Sharon said. "And I've never met you before in my life. I'm sure. I'd remember anyone who talked the way you do." *And I'm obviously dreaming, and I had better wake up before I do miss a lesson and my coach gets mad at me.*

"The ice got her," the child said with a sigh. "The Ancient said that thou wouldst not remember, but I had hoped it was mistaken. Come, I shall take thee to it, and it can explain."

"What is the Ancient?" Sharon asked, swinging her legs over the side of the bed and feeling for her slippers. Fortunately they were there—and so was her skate bag, which she had dropped next to the bed last night. Apparently whatever had brought her here had brought along everything within a few feet of her as well. She rummaged in the bag and pulled out a pair of leg warmers and a hooded sweatshirt, a souvenir of her last skating competition.

"What dost thou?" the child asked.

Sharon stared at her. "I'm putting on more clothes—what does it look like I'm doing? You must have noticed that it's cold in here."

"But that is not proper clothing!" the child protested. "The Ancient will not like it if thou comest before it looking like a..." the child's voice trailed off; obviously she was unable to find a description for what she thought Sharon looked like. "Thou art a princess, and thou must dress properly," she said earnestly. "I shall help thee," she added, picking up a dress and shawl like the ones she was wearing from the foot of the bed. "I regret that we have no servants at present—"

"Don't tell me, let me guess," Sharon said sarcastically, "the ice got them too."

The child nodded.

"Look, kid," Sharon said, "ice doesn't *get* people. Ice is just frozen water—it's not as if it could think for itself or anything."

"Thou dost not comprehend," the child said, pulling Sharon's nightshirt off over her head.

"That's the first sensible thing you've said yet," Sharon muttered, as the child dropped the dress over Sharon's head and tugged it into place. Sharon gasped as the cold fabric touched her bare skin. The child knelt behind her, laced the dress up the back, and put the matching shawl around Sharon's shoulders. Then she began to fuss with Sharon's hair, parting it in the middle and coiling it back away from Sharon's face.

The child stepped back to survey the full effect and smiled faintly. "Thou art so beautiful," she said wistfully. "I wish that I looked more like thee. Why dost thou have black hair and deep blue eyes whilst I have brown and grey?"

Sharon decided that there was already enough culture shock in the room without her trying to explain dyes that changed brown hair to black and contact lenses designed to change pale grey eyes to any color one desired. *It's a good thing I didn't get a set in purple*, she thought with some amusement. *That would probably really freak the poor kid.* She also decided against explaining about the hours she spent in the gym every day, lifting weights and exercising on the Stairmaster, so that she could keep in shape and look good to the judges at competitions. Keeping her weight down was a constant battle, and she needed to maintain a lot of muscle, both in her legs and in her upper body, in order to be able to do spins and jumps. But she didn't think she could explain a Stairmaster to this child. For all that the girl looked exactly like her, she seemed alien.

She followed the child up a flight of cold stone stairs that hugged the inner wall of the Tower. *The heat must be off in my cottage if I'm this cold in my dreams*, she thought idly. The child was breathing hard as they went up the stairs, but Sharon didn't find them particularly bothersome. Of course, Sharon was accustomed to running up and down a flight of seventy stairs to and from the rink several times a day.

They wound up in a room at the very top of the Tower. It had one small window off to the side, but mostly it was lit with candles, which were burning low and dripping wax all down the sides of the candle stands. The wall was the same grey stone as the rest of the Tower, but there was a design carved in a circle on one wall. It reminded Sharon a bit of the Celtic interlace pattern that she had seen on someone's skating dress recently. In front of the design was a wooden pedestal, and on the pedestal was a skull—apparently the skull of a saber-toothed tiger. Sharon yawned. For some reason she was very tired today, and sabertooths didn't interest her particularly. She had grown up near the La Brea Tar Pit, which was full of the darn things.

"Good morrow, Princess Morag, Princess Sharon," a voice said. It seemed to be coming from the skull, but the skull's jaws weren't moving. *And besides*, Sharon thought, *skulls can't talk—especially skulls of extinct animals too dumb to stay out of the tar pits.*

Good morrow, Ancient," the child, presumably Morag, said respectfully, apparently addressing the skull. "I have brought her here, as you instructed, but she remembers nothing."

"I warned thee that such was likely to be the case," the voice said calmly.

"She speaketh most strangely," Morag continued, sounding puzzled, "and she hath wondrous strange clothing—and black hair and blue eyes. Are you certain that she is my sister?"

"Quite certain," the voice said. "It is time that I explained matters to Princess Sharon."

There were no chairs in the room, and Sharon had the feeling this was going to be a long story. She shrugged and flopped into a sitting position on the floor, leaning back against the wall opposite the skull. Morag, who was standing facing the skull with her hands clasped loosely together in front of her, cast Sharon a scandalized glance.

Sharon concluded that, once again, she had done something un-princess-like. So far the list seemed to include crying, dressing in clothing warm enough to prevent frostbite, and sitting on the floor. When she was growing up, Sharon had always dreamed of being a princess and living in a castle. Now she was rapidly concluding that being a princess was a drag and life in a castle was cold and uncomfortable. She wondered where the bathroom was, and if they ever ate around here. Probably the skull didn't, but Morag appeared to be a growing girl and thus presumably in need of food.

"Did Princess Morag tell thee about the ice?" the skull asked.

"She said that it 'got' her mother and all the servants," Sharon replied. "That doesn't make sense to me."

Morag shuddered. "Ice is so strong and so smooth—there's nothing one can do to it."

Sharon giggled. "Strong and smooth? Ice?" She shook her head. "You've obviously never seen a rink after a freestyle session—between the toe-pick marks from jump take offs and the grooves in the ice from the landings, it's a real mess. I've seen little kids kick holes the size of my fist in the ice without even trying." She shrugged, and continued, "And of course, heat will melt it right back into water."

"Unfortunately," the skull said, "we do not get enough heat here now to melt ice."

"You mean you're having an ice age?" Sharon asked. "Glaciers coming out of the north and stuff like that?"

"No," the skull said. "Once, long ago, that did happen here. But now we have a different problem. We have a mage who can control the ice."

"And he's using it to kill everyone?" Sharon asked. "Isn't that sort of wasteful? I mean, can he cook? If he kills all the servants, he'll have to, won't he? Cook, and do his own laundry, and clean the castle..."

The skull interrupted her. "It is thy destiny to stop him. That is why thou wert fostered in the other world, so that thou wouldst learn the powers needed to defeat him. The Queen thy Mother foresaw this day."

"Thou hast twice my years," Princess Morag pointed out, "so thou must know many more spells that I do. I have studied all my life, but doubtless thou hast twice my knowledge."

"You mean magic?" Sharon looked at her incredulously. "We don't study magic in my world. Most people don't even believe it exists."

"Don't believe in magic?" Morag exclaimed in horror. "Ancient, how can a world without magic exist?"

"Calm thyself, Princess," the skull said sternly. Morag gulped and composed her features. "Princess Sharon's world has magic; they simply call it other things."

"Like what?" Sharon challenged it.

"Religion."

"You mean like witchcraft?" Sharon shook her head emphatically. "No way! I'm a Christian, not a witch."

"Dost thou attend Mass?" the skull asked.

"Of course I do!" Sharon said indignantly. "Every week."

"And thou dost not consider that to be magic? The Christian Mass is a very powerful act of ritual magic. Dost thou not feel different after receiving communion?"

Sharon had to think about that—she had always taken the effects of the sacrament for granted. "Well, yes, but—"

"Different how?" Morag asked eagerly.

"Stronger... happier... more in harmony with the world and the people around me... closer to God..." Sharon had never tried to put it into words before. "I just feel better, that's all."

"Then thou *dost* know what magic is and what it feels like," the Ancient said. "With that and the physical strength and skills thou hast, thou canst accomplish the task before thee."

"What task is that?" Sharon asked warily.

"When the Queen died," the skull explained, "the mage took her orb. He cannot use it, but as long as he keeps it away from Princess Morag, she cannot use it either. And she needs it if she is to survive."

"What's an orb?" Sharon asked.

"It is what gives the Queen her power," the skull explained. "It is what makes her the Queen."

"What about the King?" Sharon inquired.

"What is a king?" Morag asked.

I've heard of sheltered childhoods, Sharon thought, *but this is ridiculous.* "The Queen's husband," she said. Morag still looked blank. "Our father. What happened to him?"

"Father?" Morag didn't seem to know that word either.

"You don't have a father," the skull said. "The Queen bears her daughters alone."

"Parthenogenesis?" Sharon asked incredulously.

"Yes," the skull replied.

"So that's why my hair and eye color bothers you," Sharon said, turning to Morag. "I'm supposed to look exactly like you, just older, right?"

"Yes," Morag said nervously. "Why dost thou not?"

"I'm a skater," Sharon explained, "and I skate in competitions, where part of what they judge you on is how you look. So I changed my hair and eye color to be more striking, and I work really hard to stay thin so that I'll look good in my costumes. If I didn't dye my hair and wear lenses that change my eye color, I would look just like you."

"Truly?"

"Yes, truly. When I was ten, I looked exactly the way you do now."

"So thou truly art my sister." Morag sounded immensely relieved.

"It looks that way." Sharon smiled reassuringly at the child.

"If thou lookest unlike Princess Morag and the Queen," the skull said, "that should help in thy quest. The mage will not immediately recognize the for what thou art."

"Probably not," Sharon said. "Is he likely to try to kill me if he does?"

"He will try to kill thee in any case," the skull said. "He has killed everyone who has left this Tower. But his powers are weaker by day, so if thou canst get the orb back here by nightfall, thou shouldst survive."

This is definitely the strangest dream I've ever had in my life. "Where is the orb, and what does it look like?" she asked.

"The Queen our Mother took it to the Temple," Morag said. "Yesterday was the longest day, when the orb is taken to the Temple to soak in the sunlight. The orb is a sphere, about this big," she held up her small hands, indicating something about two inches in diameter, "and it is made of translucent green stone."

"So you think the orb is still at the Temple?" Sharon asked.

Morag nodded. "I know it is. I can feel it; I have been able to ever since Mother died. I would know if it had been moved."

"So how do I find the Temple?" Sharon asked. "How far away is it?" She moved to look out the small window. The Tower was surrounded by a sea of ice as far as she could see, as if it were set in the middle of an enormous rink.

"I do not know." Morag looked confused. "Canst thou not feel it?"

"Feel what?" Sharon asked, feeling as confused as Morag looked. "The Temple? The orb?" She frowned. "If you can't tell me how to find it, you'll have to come with me and show me. Can you skate?"

"What is skating?" Morag asked.

"Princess Morag cannot leave the Tower," the skull said firmly. "I shall have to link you together. Princess Sharon, come touch the top of my skull, right behind my eye socket."

Sharon looked dubiously at it, then shrugged. *What can an old skull do to me, even if it can talk?* She gingerly touched the tip of her index finger to the skull. It felt as if a strong electric current was running through her, from the top of her head and the soles of her feet through her finger and into the skull. She tried to pull her hand away, but she couldn't move at all. Suddenly this seemed less like a dream and more like a very strange reality.

"Princess Morag," the skull said. Its voice seemed to echo inside Sharon's head. Then Morag touched the skull, and Sharon abruptly realized what it had meant by 'link together.' She was looking at the skull through two sets of eyes, until she hastily squeezed her own shut, leaving her looking across the skull from Morag's viewpoint and giving her an excellent view of her terrified face.

"Fear not, Sharon." She heard Morag's voice in her head, and she knew that neither of them was moving her lips. "Open thine eyes."

Sharon cautiously opened her eyes to narrow slits. As she did so, her vision through Morag's eyes went away. She opened her eyes the rest of the way, and discovered that the feeling in her body was returning to normal and she could move again. She backed cautiously away from the skull.

"The link is in place," Morag said. "Thank you, Ancient." She bowed slightly to the skull.

"Uh, thanks," Sharon added. *I think.*

"Come, Sharon," Morag took her hand and dragged her toward the stairs. "If thou art to return by dark, thou must leave very soon."

The girls went down the stairs together, much faster than they had come up them. Morag was obviously in a hurry now. "Canst thou feel the orb now?" she asked.

Sharon concentrated as much as she could while hurrying down the stairs. "I can feel something out that way," she admitted, pointing, "but I'm not sure what it is."

"That is the correct direction," Morag said. "And now I can see what thou seest and speak to thee without speaking aloud, so I can tell thee the way if thou losest it."

"About this wizard—" Sharon began.

"Mage," Morag corrected her.

"Whatever. What are his weaknesses? Is there any way to kill him?"

"He liketh not sunlight and warmth," Morag said, "but, beyond that, I do not know." She looked anxiously up at Sharon. "I hope that thou wilt not encounter him."

"Me too." They reached the room where Sharon's bed was. "I'm going to get dressed," she said. "Can you fix me some food to take with me? I haven't had anything to eat since dinner last night, and I'm starved!"

"Fasting makes our link stronger," Morag said.

"Skating with no food makes me fall down a lot," Sharon pointed out. "You can fast if you want, since you're staying here, but I'm going to be out there moving around and using energy. I need food."

"Very well," Morag agreed. "I shall fetch thee some bread." She left the room and continued down the stairs.

"Well, bread is better than nothing," Sharon sighed, "but it's certainly enough to make me appreciate the food back at the training center. I wonder if they can send me back when I've got the orb for them." She dropped the shawl on the bed and tried to get out of the dress. "For that matter, I wonder if I can unlace this wretched dress." She struggled unsuccessfully with it for several minutes before Morag came back with a tray.

"Here," she said, handing Sharon a hunk of bread. It was lumpy and coarse, but Sharon was too hungry to care. "I'll unlace the dress for thee," Morag continued. She had it undone before Sharon could take more than three bites of bread.

Sharon set the bread aside, dumped her skate bag on the bed, and began to select and hastily put on clothing. Even though it must be almost noon, it was still very cold in the room. She pulled on a pair of beige tights and a skating dress that so horrified Morag by its short skirt and bright colors that her thoughts came through to Sharon even though she wasn't deliberately projecting them.

"No, Morag," Sharon explained, "a virgin in my world can wear colors other than white. The color of my clothing says nothing at all about my character or my morals."

She put on the hooded sweatshirt with a pocket across its front, shoved her gloves in the pocket for the moment, and sat down on the edge of the bed to lace on her skates. Since the blades were covered by plastic guards, she could walk on them indoors, and it was certainly easier to put them on while sitting on a bed than it would be sitting on the ice outside the Tower door.

She shoved her water bottle, which was almost completely full, and all the bread she could fit into the pocket, picked up the piece she had been eating, and headed toward the stairs. "All right, Morag, show me the way out of here."

Morag led her down the rest of the stairs to a small door at the base of the Tower. She opened it, and the ice stretched out in front of Sharon. In spite of the seriousness of the situation, Sharon smiled. The ice was flat and smooth, just the way she liked it. She removed her blade guards and crammed them in next to her water bottle as she stepped carefully onto the ice. She skated a few curves to see how this ice felt against her blades, and smiled at Morag. "It's good ice," she said reassuringly, "hard and fast. I should be able to make good time to the Temple."

"I'll stay linked and keep watch," Morag promised. "Be careful."

Sharon stroked towards the Temple. The land was almost completely level, so it wasn't very different from being on a rink, except that this 'rink' really did seem to go on forever. She looked back at the Tower to see how far she had come and gasped in surprise. She knew that Tower. It was part of an old ruin called The Castle, not far from the Training Center. The Tower was the only part of the ruin that still stood, and there were all sorts of rumors about the place: that it had been an insane asylum, or a sanitarium for patients with tuberculosis, or that Satanists still used it for their rituals. Sharon had been there a few times with her boyfriend John, but only once at night. At night, it was a spooky place.

"Sharon?" Morag's voice whispered in her head. "Is something amiss?"

"Amiss?" It took Sharon a second to place the word. "No, Morag, it's okay. Nothing's wrong. The Tower just looks familiar, that's all—there's one like it in my world."

"It is probably one of the gates between our worlds," Morag thought calmly.

Sharon decided she didn't want to think about gates between worlds at the moment. She turned her back on the Tower and continued toward the Temple, chewing on another piece of bread as she skated. By the time she saw the Temple in front of her, she had finished all the bread and about half her water, but the food had made her feel better. Her legs ached slightly from all the stroking, but not enough to inconvenience her.

As she came to the final approach to the Temple, she heard a gasp of horror in her head. Looking at what lay ahead, she could understand it. There was a deep gorge between her and the Temple, and the only bridge across it was about three inches wide—and at least fifteen feet long. She could feel terror well up inside her, but she realized that most of it was not hers. "Morag, relax," she thought at her little sister. "This is nothing to be afraid of."

"What if you fall?" It was the wail of a terrified child.

"I'm not going to fall. I've had to do harder things than this on beginning tests, and I've passed senior level." She backed up a bit so that she could get up to speed; there wasn't going to be any way to cheat on this maneuver. "I've had to do a spiral on a flat edge for at least four times my body length, and this is only about three."

"What's a spiral?"

"Just watch." Sharon pushed off strongly. Left, right, left, right. She hit the bridge in a perfect flat spiral position, right foot even on both edges of her skate blade, chest and left leg parallel to the ice, with the left leg turned out from the hip and the toe pointed, head up and facing into the breeze created by the air she was moving through, and arms outstretched to the sides, arching her chest slightly. It was definitely one of the best spirals she had ever done, and it carried her smoothly over the bridge in the space of a single breath. As soon as she reached the Temple entrance, an area about three feet square, she dropped her left foot to the ice, pulled her arms in, and converted her remaining momentum into a two-foot spin. She stopped it with a toe-pick into the ice, and threw back her head, laughing softly in delight. "That felt good!" she thought.

"Yes," Morag's thoughts were wistful, "it did."

Sharon skated to the doorway and looked at the stone floor of the Temple, then up at the sun, which was halfway down to the horizon. *I'd better hurry*, she thought. Picking up her right foot, she ran her fingers along the blade to remove the excess ice, then pulled the blade guards from her pocket and fitted one over the right blade. She repeated the procedure with her left skate and walked into the Temple.

She passed through a small anteroom and into the main hall, which had a skylight in the center of the ceiling. On an altar under the skylight a woman lay on her back, holding a green sphere in her cupped hands. There sphere glowed faintly in the sunlight, despite the fact that both woman and sphere were covered with at least an inch of ice."

Sharon didn't need Morag's cry of "Mother" bouncing through her skull to recognize the woman. *That's what I'd look like*, she realized, *if I weren't a skater*. The woman's eyes were closed, but Sharon had no doubt they were the same pale grey as hers and Morag's. The brown hair, with a few strands of white mixed in, was parted in the center and coiled back as Morag had tried to do with Sharon's—which had come loose while she was skating and now hung every which way about her head. The woman looked peaceful, like an illustration of Sleeping Beauty or Snow White in a book of fairy tales.

"Are you sure she's dead?" Sharon wondered.

"Hast thou never seen a dead body before?" Morag sounded surprised.

"Well, no, never," Sharon admitted.

"Look at her arms," Morag instructed. "See how her hands and forearms are white, but the backs of her upper arms look bruised? After death, the blood flows to the lowest part of the body and stays there. She's dead, and she's been dead since last night. I felt her die." Sharon felt a faint flicker of emotional pain, quickly covered by annoyance. "Just get the orb and get out of there, before the mage finds you!"

Sharon frowned at the orb. The Queen was not grasping it; it rested on top of her open hands, but it was still covered with ice, and there was nothing in the room to chip it out with. *Nothing except my skate blades*, Sharon thought. She removed the guard from her right blade, put her gloves on so that she could hold onto the ice-covered body for balance, and swung her leg over the body. A few good whacks with the heel of her blade chipped away the ice that held the orb in place at the bottom, but most of it was still covered with ice when she pulled it free. She shoved it into her pocket and put her blade guard back on. "What about our mother's body?" she thought to Morag.

"Leave it," Morag replied, "just get back here as quickly as thou canst!"

Nonetheless, Sharon bowed her head over the body for a moment and said a quick prayer for the repose of the Queen's soul. Then she walked quickly out of the Temple.

She frowned as she looked at the bridge. With the small patch of ice on this side, she didn't think she could get up enough speed to be sure of getting back across it in a spiral. And it was too narrow to crawl along. *A balance beam is wider*, Sharon thought in disgust. *How do people usually get in and out of here?*

She would just have to sit straddled across it and pull herself along with her hands. That would be slow and a bit precarious, especially for the contents of her pocket. She pulled out the ice-covered orb and gritted her teeth. There was no help for it; the safest place for the orb was down the front of her skating dress. If she tied the neck of her sweatshirt tightly, the orb would stay with her even if she wound up hanging upside down. She loosened the neck of the sweatshirt and quickly shoved the orb down the front of her dress, tucking it under the waistband of her tights. The cold made her eyes fill with tears, but at least it was secure now. She pulled up the hood of her sweatshirt and tied the drawstring at the neck.

Dragging herself across the 'bridge' seemed to take forever, but eventually she crawled onto the ice at the other side, moved away from the gorge, stood up, and started stroking back to the Tower.

The sun was halfway below the horizon as she approached the Tower, and Morag had been getting steadily more agitated for the past half-hour. Now she continually urged Sharon to hurry, and Sharon was getting a headache. "Can't you be quiet?" she thought, trying to project reassurance. "You're starting to make *me* nervous!"

"He's coming," Morag whispered. "I can feel him."

"Damn!" Sharon muttered. The ice was starting to crack around her, and a two-foot-wide fissure opened up in her path, between her and the Tower.

She remembered her coach teaching her a jump called a Falling Leaf. "Pretend you're jumping over a mud puddle," he had said. She turned quickly to glide backwards on two feet toward the fissure, pushing a couple of times with the side of one foot to build up speed. Just before she reached it, she twisted her head and upper body to the left to look behind her and picked up her left foot and held it at the back of her right ankle. As she reached the very edge of the fissure, she jumped off her right foot, reaching out with her left foot and both arms. While she didn't think this jump had quite the graceful floating quality of a falling leaf that its originator had in mind, it did get her safely into the Tower courtyard.

Then Morag's voice in her head said in warning. "He's here!"

The sun was almost completely below the horizon by now, but Sharon had excellent night vision. (The lamps on the stairway down from the rink were always getting broken, so she had plenty of practice in navigating hazardous terrain with almost no light.) She could see the man standing on the doorstep to the Tower, even though he was dressed in black. Black leather boots went up to his knees, black trousers were tucked into them, and he wore a black silk blouse slit open almost to his waist. Obviously the cold didn't bother him.

He looked to Sharon like a cross between the latest in teenage fashion and the cover of a romance novel, which meant that she didn't feel the automatic fear of him that Morag obviously did. Besides, it was late, she was tired, cold, and hungry; and he was between her and her dinner and bed. She pushed off hard onto her left foot on an outside edge which started her arcing away from him to his left. She prayed that he didn't know enough about skating to realize that the track she was on was going to take her right to him. Although she was moving as quickly as she could, time seemed to slow down, as if she were doing this in slow motion. She leaned into her edge, bending her left knee as deeply as she could, and stretched forward into a position similar to the spiral she had used earlier, except that this time her left arm was directly in front of her left knee. She raised her head just enough to be sure that he wasn't trying to get out of her way, but he stood unmoving, looking amused. When she was almost close enough for her hand to touch him, she snapped her left arm back and rose up on her knee, putting her body into what would have been a beautiful camel spin—if she hadn't hit him squarely in the sternum with the toe-picks of her right skate.

Sharp pointed stainless steel met bare flesh. His screams were deafening. Sharon had seen people get spiked with a skate blade before (it didn't happen often, thank God, but it did happen occasionally), but this was the first time she had ever heard anyone howl as if he were being burned alive.

She picked herself up from the ice, where she had landed on her hands and knees when her momentum was halted so abruptly, and twisted to look at him. Oddly enough, he did seem to be being burned alive. What she could see of his skin was cracking and bubbling, radiating out from where her skate blade had hit him. She watched in bewilderment as his screams died away and his entire body turned into a pile of ashes.

When she was certain he was no longer a threat, she put her blade guards back on, stepped over the pile of empty clothes, and went into the Tower, where Morag had been hovering just inside the door waiting for her.

"Is he dead?"

"It certainly looks that way." Sharon untied the neck of her sweatshirt and fished the orb out of the front of her skating dress. The ice covering it was down to a thin film in most places except for the bottom, which was bare. "Here's your orb, little sister." She handed it to Morag, then stripped off her gloves. Let's go upstairs; I want to get out of my skates and into some dry clothing. She led the way up to her room. Morag followed her, cradling the orb and gazing at it as if it held the mysteries of the universe.

Sharon stripped off her skating clothes and, for lack of anything else to wear, put the white dress on again. Morag set the orb down long enough to lace the dress for her, then resumed her study of it. Sharon pulled her towel out of the pile of stuff on the bed and carefully dried her skate blades, then put terry cloth soakers on them to keep them from getting nicked when she put them back in her bag. She hung her wet dress, tights, and sweatshirt over the foot board of the bed.

Morag stood up abruptly. "We have to go see the Ancient."

"All right," Sharon said. "I want to ask if it knows why the mage burned up like that."

She followed Morag up the stairs again, back to the room at the top of the Tower. By now the skull looked like a old friend. "Good evening, Ancient," she said. "Do you know what happened to the mage?"

"I could feel something," it replied. "Tell me."

Sharon described what she had seen to the best of her ability. "Why did he burn up like that?" she finished.

"What are thy skate blades make of?" the skull asked.

"Stainless steel."

"Does this 'steel' have iron in it?"

Sharon frowned. "I think so. Why?"

"The mage must have had elven blood," the skull said. "Elves are the only creatures I have ever heard of that burn when exposed to iron. Didst thou hit him hard enough to draw blood?"

"I couldn't see blood through the burns," Sharon said, "but I must have. Toe picks are sharp and I hit him hard on bare skin."

"That would carry the iron burn through his entire body then," the skull concluded. "Thou hast done well."

Sharon bit her lip. "I've never killed anyone before—and I didn't mean to kill him. Murder is a mortal sin."

"I think if you ask your priest, he will tell you that elves do not have souls," the skull said soothingly. "Therefore, killing him was no more murder than killing a venomous spider."

"Oh." That made Sharon feel a bit better. "So what happens to me now?"

"Dost thou wish to stay here?" the skull asked. "Now that the mage is gone, the ice should melt and the land will be fair once again."

Sharon thought about it. She was a princess and she could stay here in the Tower and be a princess. But if the ice melted, she would have no place to skate, and even if it didn't, her coach and her friends were all back in her own world. And in this world she had no father and her mother was dead, and she had no memories of her mother save as a dead body. In her own world, she had parents who loved her, even if they weren't her biological parents. And in her own world she had her boyfriend, while here they would probably expect her to reproduce by parthenogenesis—assuming that she was allowed to have children at all. She might be a princess, but Morag was to be Queen. Morag was a nice kid, but the idea of life with only Morag and a talking skull for company was a bit daunting. "I want to go home," Sharon said, "back to my own world."

"Very well," the skull replied. "Morag can send you back as soon as she masters the orb."

"How long will that take?" Sharon looked at Morag, who was frowning down at the orb.

"I fear it is broken," Morag said. "I cannot feel anything from it."

"What?" Sharon yelped. "After what I went through to get that thing, it had better not be broken! Let me see it." She lifted the orb out of Morag's unresisting hands—and nearly dropped it, as a flood of emotions and images swept through her. She shoved it back into Morag's hands and dropped to the floor, putting her head between her knees and hoping she wasn't going to faint. She had never felt so dizzy in her life, even when she first started learning to do spins.

"Morag," she said firmly. "That orb is *not* broken."

"Then why do I feel nothing from it?"

"Ancient?" Sharon appealed to the skull.

"I cannot help you with this," the skull replied. "Morag must master the orb herself—or thou must."

Sharon frowned as she looked at Morag. "You don't feel anything from the orb?" Morag shook her head. "What do you feel?" Sharon asked. "Not from the orb—from anyplace, from inside yourself."

"Nothing." Morag looked blank and tired. "What am I supposed to feel?"

"What did you feel when you realized your mother was dead?"

"I knew I had to get the orb. That's why we brought you here."

"No," Sharon said. "You're missing the point. Not what did you *do*, what did you *feel*."

"A Princess does not cry," Morag said, as if by rote. "A Princess does not let feelings get in the way of what must be done."

"Maybe it's different for a Queen," Sharon suggested. "Maybe your lack of feelings is what's keeping you from feeling the orb."

"So how am I supposed to feel?" Morag asked.

"You know," Sharon said. "You're just fighting it. Stop fighting your feelings, and the orb will work for you just fine." She fought unsuccessfully to keep from yawning. "I've had a long day," she said. "I'm going to bed. You might try that too; sleep might help you. Good night, Morag. Good night, Ancient."

Good night, Princess Sharon," the skull said.

Sharon stumbled off to bed. She was too tired to struggle with the task of unlacing the white gown, so she slept in it.

Sometime in the early hours of the morning, Sharon woke up. Morag was standing next to the bed, crying her eyes out. "My mother is dead," she sobbed. Sharon sat up, reached out and put her arms around the child.

"I know," she said, starting to cry herself.

"I know how to use the orb now," Morag sobbed. "But it hurts! And I shall have to use it to send thee home, and I shall miss thee!"

Sharon held Morag and rocked her in her arms until the girl fell asleep, then lay down next to her and went back to sleep herself.

Her alarm was ringing, and it was barely dawn. Sharon sat up in bed, switched off the alarm, and put saline solution in her eyes. *Boy, that was a weird dream*, she thought. Then she looked down at the white dress she was still wearing, at her skating cloths and sweatshirt hanging on the footboard of the bed, and at the mess that had been a neatly packed skating bag. *It wasn't a dream, she realized, and I'm going to be late for my session if I don't hurry. And if I do hurry, I'll have time to eat breakfast first.*

That was incentive. With concentration and the use of the large mirror in the bathroom, she managed to get out of the dress unaided. She threw on the first clean skating outfit that came to hand, ran a brush through her hair, and put a skirt over her skating dress so that she could go to breakfast. As she ate a double helping of pancakes with lots of syrup, she noted the date on the morning news show playing on the television. *I haven't lost a day*, she discovered with relief. *That's good, I can explain why I'm so tired much more easily than I can explain why I was missing for 24 hours.*

She dragged herself through her day's skating, then called John. "Can you take me over to The Castle this evening?" she asked him. "There's something I want to see there."

"Yeah, sure."

John came for her right after dinner, and they went to the old Tower. It was dark by then, so they didn't get too close. But they were close enough for Sharon to see Morag standing next to the window in the middle of the Tower, holding the orb and smiling down at her.

BLOOD CALLS TO BLOOD

Lucy arrived home from work wanting nothing more than a long hot bath and a quiet evening. It was good to be back on the streets after a rotation in Juvenile. Juvenile was a tough assignment, especially when you had children of your own; it made you only too aware of all the awful things that happened to children in this world. But walking a beat, or, in Lucy's case, bicycling it, was hot and physically tiring.

She could hear voices coming from the kitchen, presumably one or more of the children, but she didn't go that way. They knew that she had just come in; her home security system was the best that money could buy and thirteen-year-old hackers could improve upon, and she had passed three cameras already. But, by family custom, nobody spoke to Mom when she got home from work until after she'd had a bath and a chance to unwind. So Lucy continued unmolested upstairs to the master bedroom, took off her gunbelt, unloaded the gun and locked it away, shed her clothes and the bulletproof vest, and started filling the tub. The attached bathroom boasted a tub that would hold several people (assuming, of course, that they were very good friends). The tub also had a built-in Jacuzzi. Lucy climbed in, turned on the jets, and soaked until she had dishpan hands, feet, knees, and elbows.

Feeling considerably more human, she put on a robe and went downstairs to join the rest of the family for dinner. She found her husband George and their twin daughters, Diana and Cynthia, at the kitchen table. There was no sign of dinner. Piles of reference books surrounded them, and all three were busily reading. She picked up the nearest book. "*Elf Defense?*" she asked incredulously, noting the title.

Diana, who at age fifteen was already showing the makings of a fine reference librarian, looked up. "Well, hard data on this problem is a bit difficult to find. After all, Mom, not that many people really believe in elves these days. That's why we didn't call the police."

"When?" Lucy said hollowly, "and about what? And where's Michael? Is he spending the night at Jimmy's?"

Cynthia seemed totally engrossed in the book she was studying, which, Lucy, reading upside down, saw was titled *Psychic Self-Defense*. Diana looked at her father, who also looked as if he would rather not answer that question.

"Maybe you should sit down, dear," he said.

Lucy grabbed the nearest chair and sat. "All right, I'm sitting down. "Where's Michael?"

"He was kidnapped by elves this afternoon."

Lucy shot back to her feet. "Elves?"

"Now you can see why we didn't feel that calling the police would be appropriate," George said.

"We didn't want to be laughed at," Cynthia added, looking up from her book.

"I'm not laughing," Lucy pointed out. "Start talking."

"I wasn't here," Cynthia said quickly. "I was still at the hospital." She did volunteer work there three afternoons a week.

"And Daddy was writing," Diana said. This meant that Daddy's brain had been in another universe at the time. "So I guess I'm your only witness, Mother."

"All right, then, Diana. What happened?"

"Do you remember Precious? That girl last month with datura poisoning?"

"How could I forget Precious Gift of the Goddess? It's not an easy name to fit on bureaucratic forms. But, as far as I know, she's in foster care now, so it's hard to see how she could have anything to do with this."

"Maybe you should see the note." Diana handed over a small parchment scroll. Lucy unrolled it. It was written in silver ink, real silver, judging by the weight of it.

The handwriting was spiky and obviously intended to look elvish in origin, but Lucy had been born with the Sight. This note was written by a human, a very angry human.

"You took my last-born from me," she read aloud, "so I have taken yours. The fair folk will not be cheated." She frowned at the signature. "'Morgana.' Are we talking about Precious's grandmother here?"

"Is her name Morgana?" Diana asked in surprise. "I though it was Janine."

"She calls herself Morgana," Lucy said, "and she's definitely a mortal. So where do the elves come in?"

"They took Michael," Diana said, "and they left this note."

"What makes you think they were elves?"

"They opened a gate," Diana pointed out into the yard, "right there, next to the hummingbird feeder." Lucy looked. There was definitely a gate in the back yard, a hole in the side of the hill with a silvery grey light coming from it. The light turned reddish at ground level, and Lucy, squinting, saw that the red area was just above one of her good cast iron skillets. She could feel a faint pull though it as well, a tugging at the bond that stretched between her and each of her children. Since Diana and Cynthia were in the kitchen with her, Michael was obviously on the other side of that gate.

Diana continued with her story. "They came in here and grabbed Michael—we were sitting at the table. He broke his glass against the table and tried to slice them with the broken edges, but it was like it didn't touch them—"

"Are you sure it did?"

"—but I hit one of them in the face with the serving spoon I got at RenFaire, and the handle left a burn mark." She pointed to the spoon in question: a copper bowl riveted to a wrought iron handle. "A human would have been marked by both the copper and iron, not just the iron, and he would have been cut or bruised, not burned." She shuddered. "And you should have heard him scream! They bolted back through the gate faster than I could move. I threw the skillet at them, but I missed. Mom, I'm sorry; I tried, I really did!" She burst into tears, and Lucy reached over and grabbed her in a hug.

"I know you did, honey, and this isn't your fault." She patted her sobbing daughter on the back. "Don't worry. We'll get Michael back." She looked out the window again. "Besides, you may not have hit them, but you appear to have locked their gate open. That will make going after them much easier."

"I found it!" Cynthia said suddenly, and Diana pulled away from Lucy and grabbed at the book. Diana had always been good at blocking her emotions with her intellect.

"Great!" She scanned the page quickly. "We'll need salt. Daddy, do we have any sea salt left?"

"Third cupboard from the left," George said automatically. "What did you find?"

"The formula for making holy water." Diana said. "According to my research, such as it is, iron and holy water are the main weapons against elves."

"Actually, Coke works, too," Cynthia said. "At least it did on Precious. She got a can of it while she was in the hospital and it really *did* make her drunk. And she says she's only part elf."

"Getting someone drunk isn't much of a weapon," Diana pointed out, pulling several two-liter soda bottles from the recycling bin. "And first you'd have to get all of them to drink Coke—and you can't count on their having watched enough TV advertising for that."

"Iron," Cindy stared into space, obviously trying to think of good sources of iron. "Would steel count?"

"I should think so," George said. "It's an alloy of iron."

"Are you going after them, Mom?" Cindy asked, eyeing Lucy as if measuring her.

"Yes, I am." *At least I've been Under the Hill before,* Lucy thought, *even if it was years and years ago. And the elves generally don't hurt children, so Michael should be okay for a while anyway.*

"Then I've got the perfect thing for you to wear," Cindy said. She ran from the room to fetch whatever it was. Diana had filled a large mixing bowl with water and was now casting salt into it, murmuring prayers as she did. Lucy waited until she had finished the process and was pouring the water into the empty soda bottles.

"Diana, why did you say Morgana's name was Janine?"

Diana looked at her and bit her lip. "I did some research at the county courthouse, after Cindy first met Precious. I didn't mean to pry into your private life, Mother, but Precious said that she and Cindy had the same blood, and I was curious."

"The files at the courthouse are a matter of public record, Diana; it's hardly prying into my private life. Putting a camera in my bedroom is prying into my private life."

George smothered a laugh. "I think Michael understands that now."

"He had better," Lucy said. "So, Diana, what did you find out?"

"I started with Precious's birth certificate, which took a while to find because it was under 'Goddess, Precious G.' Her mother's name is Laurel, and for father it says 'unknown.' So I looked up Laurel's birth certificate, and it says father unknown, but the mother is Janine Kennedy. I had brought our family genealogy notebook with me, and when I checked your birth certificate the mother's name was the same and the age was right. So it looks as though Precious is our first cousin."

"As far as I know, that's correct," Lucy said. "You never met your grandmother; she didn't approve of my career choice or my choice of husband. As far as I'm concerned, she's no loss. Dad left her when I was ten, but I had to visit her until I turned eighteen."

"Do you think she might have Michael at her house?" Diana asked. "I've got a recent address for her."

"How recent?"

"Last summer. She changed her voter registration, to switch political parties. She's registered as Peace and Freedom at the moment. It looks like she changes every few years—her deleted registration wasn't very old either, but her address hasn't changed since Laurel was born."

"It hasn't changed since *I* was born," Lucy said. "Her father left her the house and a trust fund. It's too bad; if she'd ever had to work for a living she might have had to learn to interact with mundane reality. Then at least she might have told her granddaughter that datura is poisonous." She sighed. "But once she finished school and married, she sort of pulled away from the real world. She was more interested in elves than people for as long as I can remember. It drove Dad nuts, and Laurel's birth was the last straw."

"Laurel really isn't his, then," Diana said. "Is that why he divorced her?"

"Diana!" For the first time in this conversation Lucy was shocked. "Of course he didn't divorce her! Divorce is wrong. You know that—or didn't they cover that in confirmation class?"

"Yes, they did, and I know it's wrong, but lots of Catholics still get divorced, and if she was committing adultery, that's a mortal sin." Diana giggled suddenly. "And if she had a child by an elf, that's miscegenation."

"What's miscegenation?" Cindy asked, coming into the room carrying a double handful of what looked like a pile of small metal rings.

"Mixing of races, in this case interbreeding between human and elf," Lucy replied briskly. "What do you have there?"

"So Precious really is part elf?" Cindy asked. Diana nodded. "Well I guess it's better to have an elf for a father than to have a mother so promiscuous that she can't say who fathered her child." She spread the metal out on the table. Lucy looked at it incredulously.

"You're joking, right?"

"No, Mom, really. It's stainless steel, and Dad says that counts as iron, and I'm sure it will fit you. We're pretty close to the same size."

George coughed. "I bet it would look great on you, dear."

Lucy glared at him. "I am not going anywhere in a chain mail bikini!" She turned on Cindy. "And where did you get this, young lady? I haven't seen it before."

"At the RenFaire."

"You wore *this* at the Renaissance Faire? I'm amazed you didn't get sunstroke."

"No, I bought it at the RenFaire. I'm planning to wear it at a science fiction convention in May."

"We'll discuss *that* later," Lucy said. "But I assure you that I am not going outside the house in that. I'll wear my bulletproof vest; the breast and back plates in it are steel."

"But they're covered by fabric," Cindy protested.

"That doesn't matter as long as it's not silk," Diana said. "Silk insulates, but I don't think Kevlar does."

"I still think she'd be better off in this," Cindy said.

"Not if I have to come out by another gate somewhere else," Lucy pointed out. "I'd be arrested for indecent exposure, or at least picked up for psychiatric evaluation." She scooped up the chain mail. "Put this back in your room, Cindy."

Cindy took the bikini, but stood there frowning. "Maybe if you drink holy water it will help protect you."

"Salt water is an emetic," Lucy pointed out. "I don't think that throwing up would improve my efficiency."

"I can fix that," Cindy said. "I'll be right back." She dashed out of the room again.

Lucy sighed. "While Cindy has her next brilliant idea, I'll go get dressed." She went back to her room, dressed in blue jeans, sneakers, a t-shirt, her vest, and a sweat shirt. She stuffed her keys and ID into one pocket and looked at the gun drawer. *No*, she decided, *it probably won't help against elves, and if I shoot it I'll spend days doing paperwork. And it would be impossible to explain the circumstances to a review board.* She took the handcuffs off her belt and shoved them in another pocket and picked up her police-issue flashlight before returning to the kitchen.

In her absence the girls had gathered together Michael's water pistol collection, and Diana and George were filling all of them with holy water. Cindy was mixing something in a pitcher. She sampled a spoonful of it, then nodded. "This is it." She poured a glass of the liquid and handed it to Lucy. "Here, Mom, drink this."

"What is it?" Lucy eyed the glass suspiciously.

"Oral rehydration fluid," Cindy explained. "It's what they give babies who've lost a lot of fluid. In addition to water and salt (holy water in this case) it has baking soda and sugar. It won't make you throw up, and it should help spread the holy water throughout your body."

"I don't believe this," Lucy said. "The scientific method as applied to search and rescue operations Under the Hill." She drank down the liquid in a long gulp.

"I think it's working," Cindy said, watching her. "You look brighter somehow, sort of a glow." She grabbed a sports bottle and filled it from the pitcher. "Take this with you, and give some to Michael when you find him."

It was working all right; Lucy could feel it, and when she looked at her hands she saw that Cindy was right. Even in the daylight they glowed brightly. Also, she could feel a much stronger pull coming through the gate now. "Did Michael have any holy water with him?" she asked.

"Just one water pistol," Diana said. "He filled it at mass last Sunday. It was tucked in the back of his belt and his t-shirt covered it, so they may not have found it yet."

"Or wanted to handle it if they did find it," Lucy murmured.

Diana took a net tote bag out of the kitchen closet and started to load it. "Eight water pistols, filled. Two two-liter

ELISABETH WATERS

bottles of holy water as additional ammo. One sports bottle of potable holy water for defense. One flashlight. And the bag has both short and long handles so you can either carry it or sling it over your shoulder." She frowned anxiously. "Can anyone think of anything else?"

After a moment, three heads shook. "Okay, that's it then," Lucy said briskly, picking up the bag. "Wish me luck."

A ragged chorus of "good luck" followed her out the door.

She crossed the yard to the gate and stepped through, being careful not to touch the skillet. It seemed to be doing a fine job right where it was.

She paused just on the other side of the gate to give her eyes time to adjust to the difference in light. They were only half-adjusted when the groaning started.

"Oh, my head, my eyes!" Even through the groaning, the whispery voice was familiar, although it had been twenty-five years since Lucy had heard it.

"Moth?" she asked, bending over the slight grey figure lying at the side of the path. "What are you doing here?"

Moth whimpered and tried to shrink further into the ground. "Don't get so close! It hurts!"

"Sorry." Lucy backed off a bit. "Must be the holy water." Her eyesight was adjusting and she could see him more clearly now. He was obviously in pain, and he had a burn mark across his face. His hands were blistered as well. "What happened to your face?"

"Hit with cold iron I was," he said. Aside from the burn marks, his appearance hadn't changed since he had been one of Lucy's childhood playmates. "Do I know you, mortal?"

"I was Lucy O'Hara," she said briskly. "We used to play together when I was a child."

"And now you're a woman grown—no doubt with children of your own." Moth sighed. "You mortals grow so quickly." He looked at her and shook his head. "I remember you; you lived in the yard with the datura and the wisteria."

"Yes."

"Well, Lucy," he said in a persuasive tone only too familiar to the mother of teenagers, "could I trouble you to move that pan out of the gate?"

"The iron pan? The one that's holding the gate open?" Lucy asked in mock innocent tones.

"You always were a bright little thing." Moth admitted.

"Brighter than you, it would seem," Lucy said, "if you got tricked into tangling with my children. Why did you do it?"

"Your children?" Moth looked horrified. "The boy is yours? I swear by the Queen's throne, I had no idea. Morgana said he was hers, that he'd been kidnapped and needed to be rescued."

"My *mother* talked you into this?" Lucy was incredulous. "Don't you know she's crazy?"

Moth groaned piteously again and touched a careful finger to the burn mark on his face. "I'm certainly getting the message now. I suppose the girl that hit me was your daughter?"

Lucy nodded.

"Didn't you teach your children any manners?" he asked sternly.

"Yes, I did," Lucy said. "I also taught them that if anyone ever tried to grab them they should fight like hell."

"They're a credit to your teaching," Moth said with feeling. "Now will you please move that wretched pan so I can get this gate closed?"

"Yes, of course I will, Moth," Lucy said promptly. "Just as soon as I get Michael back and home safe. Where is he?"

"What's it worth for me to tell you?"

Lucy smiled grimly. "I haven't forgotten what I learned as a child, Moth, and I am not in a good mood right now. *You* opened this gate—for the sole purpose of kidnapping my child—and you can't leave here until the gate is closed. Obviously," she gestured to his hands, "you can't grasp the pan long enough to move it yourself, so until I come back this way with Michael, you'll be stuck here. I should think that would be reason enough for you to tell me how to find Michael as quickly as possible."

Moth ground his teeth together. "He was taken to Lord Cedric. His chamber is just the other side of the Feasting Hall. The path leads right to it."

Any path Under the Hill led to the Feasting Hall. Lucy didn't bother to ask about distance; distances Under the Hill tended to be arbitrary and changeable.

"Thank you, Moth. I'll be back as quickly as I can." She hesitated slightly. "I'm sorry my children hurt you, but my world isn't a safe place, and my children have learned to fight when they are threatened. You should not have frightened them."

Moth didn't answer, and Lucy shrugged and hurried down the path.

As she approached the Feasting Hall, she heard angry voices, punctuated with occasional screams. "Get that gun away from him!" someone cried out. Lucy pulled two water pistols out of the tote bag and slung it over her shoulder. With a pistol in each hand she stepped into the doorway.

"Freeze!" she shouted. "Police!" Mentally she groaned. *As if they're going to be impressed by the police. Some habits are so hard to break.*

"Mom!" Michael was struggling in the arms of a tall and rather beefy looking man, dressed in the silks the elf lords favored. "Shoot 'em in the face—it blinds them temporarily!" He twisted and squirted the man holding him. The man blinked and shook his head, glaring at the boy. Michael looked bewildered. Everyone else in the room froze, looking from them to Lucy and quickly back at them again.

"He's a mortal, Michael," Lucy said. "Holy water won't hurt him."

"That's right," the man said defiantly. "Nothing you can do will hurt me."

"This will hurt you plenty!" A shot rang out behind Lucy, and a bullet passed over her shoulder and buried itself in the wall above the man's head. "Let go of my brother or die!"

"Cynthia," Lucy spoke through gritted teeth, "give me the gun." She held out her right hand. Cindy, dressed in her chain mail bikini with her mother's gun belt over it, took the water pistol from Lucy's hand and replaced it with the gun.

"Mother," she spoke in an urgent whisper, "we called Precious right after you left, and she said her father is a mortal! That's why I came after you."

"And how did you get my gun and ammo?"

"Would you believe you forgot to lock it up?"

"Not for one second. We'll discuss this later, young lady."

She turned back to the man holding her child. He had pulled out a dagger and was holding it at Michael's throat. "I think we have a stand-off here, cop," he said, sneering on the last word. "Drop your gun."

"Not while you're holding a knife on my child I won't," Lucy said promptly. "Besides, if I drop the gun, it might go off again, and someone could get hurt." Cynthia edged in to her mother's right side, squirt gun at the ready, obviously prepared to deal with anyone who tried to take the gun by force.

There was a tinkling of bells as someone came through the door to Lucy's right. Lucy risked a quick glance in that direction before returning her gaze to the man who held her son. As she had suspected from the sound, it was the Queen. "Hold your fire," she murmured to Cynthia. "Do *not* shoot at anyone unless I tell you to."

"Right," Cynthia gulped, suddenly noticing that she was in over her head.

Lucy remembered the Queen as capricious, but not actively malicious. And the elves did value children. But right now the Queen's main emotion seemed to be annoyance. "What is the meaning of this disturbance?" She looked at Michael and his captor. "Lord Cedric, whence comes this child?"

"I claim him as replacement for my daughter, taken away by the police."

"You can't keep me, Michael pointed out, "I've been baptised."

"You can't be a changeling, true," Lord Cedric acknowledged, "but I can hold you hostage until my daughter is returned home."

"But she nearly got killed there!" Cindy protested.

"Does he mean Precious?" Michael asked. He twisted to look up at the man who held him. Lucy held her breath waiting to see blood drip down his neck, but apparently the knife blade wasn't tight against his throat. "You want Precious returned to *Morgana*?" Michael continued. "Are you nuts?"

Cedric glared at him. "You think she's better off in foster care, boy? I was in foster care before I came here; I know what it's like!"

"So do I!" Michael snapped. "I've been visiting her. And *she* says she's a lot happier there than she was at home!" He looked at Lucy. "If I have to stay here to keep Precious away from Morgana, Mother, I'll do it. Precious deserves better than that."

"Anybody would," Cindy said from beside Lucy. "Morgana's a psycho. Did you know that she gave Precious drugs? And she's got Laurel addicted."

Lucy sighed. "I know, Cindy. That's why Precious is in foster care."

"Why isn't Morgana in jail?" Michael demanded.

"These things take time," Lucy reminded him.

"Yeah, the wheels of justice make the mills of God look like a fast food joint."

A cynic at thirteen, Lucy thought. *What a world we're raising our children in.*

"So I'll stay here," Michael continued. "I don't want Precious hurt again."

Cedric looked at him incredulously. The Queen looked on with faint interest. Lucy decided it was time to intervene.

"Your chivalry is noted, Michael—as is your willingness to miss next week's English exam," she added with a grin. Cindy giggled. "But I think we can work out a more reasonable solution." She turned to Lord Cedric. "You don't want Precious in state-sponsored foster care, right?"

"Absolutely not. And that is non-negotiable."

"I understand. It's not an ideal solution, especially for a child with her unique heritage."

"But if he's mortal—" Michael began.

Lucy silenced him with a look. "My sister Laurel's father was not."

"That's true enough," the Queen said coldly.

Oh-oh, Lucy thought. Cindy opened her mouth; Lucy stepped on her foot. Cindy hastily shut her mouth and tried to look like a statue. Michael caught on that this was not a good time to discuss Laurel's father and shut his mouth. "I am Precious's aunt," Lucy continued, "and this can be documented with our birth certificates. I can therefore petition the court for custody of Precious, and I see no reason why the petition should not be granted. Once Precious is living in my household, you," she addressed Lord Cedric, "will be able to visit her and see for yourself that she is well and happy."

"And I suppose you want your son back now." Lord Cedric looked her straight in the eyes.

Lucy returned his stare. "Yes."

"What guarantee do I have that you will do as you say?" he asked distrustfully.

"My word," Lucy said firmly, meeting his eyes unflinchingly.

"Why should I trust your word?" he asked.

"Because *I* say so!" Both Cedric and Lucy turned in surprise at the Queen's words. "She and her children are free to leave and are to do so immediately." Cedric looked bewildered by the Queen's decision, but Lucy noticed that the Queen squinted slightly when she looked toward Lucy and Cynthia, and that the other elves were all looking elsewhere. She looked straight at Cynthia for the first time since the girl had joined them and noticed that her skin had a bright glow to it. And there was quite a lot of skin exposed. *You could light the hall with her,* Lucy realized, *and I'll bet that she's hurting their eyes. That's why the Queen wants us gone. Her idea about drinking holy water is really paying off.*

Cedric released Michael and shoved him toward Lucy. "Go then," he said, "but remember—I know where you live."

"Good," Lucy said, smiling sweetly. "Then you'll know where to visit your daughter." She slipped her gun carefully into its holster on Cindy's hip, put her arms around her children, and herded them up the path, back to the mortal world and home, pausing only long enough at the gate to retrieve her cast-iron skillet and say goodbye to Moth.

Lucy came home from work feeling pretty good. It had been a beautiful day, nothing had gone wrong during her shift, and life was going well at home. George had just sold another book, her children were all doing well in school, and Precious had settled into the family and was catching up on the things she had missed, like ice cream and television. Precious had also proved to have quite a green thumb (or maybe a bit of outside help) and the garden was in full bloom. Lucy walked around the house, admiring the wisteria that covered the back arbor with purple flowers.

The wisteria, however was not the only thing in the back yard. Michael and Precious sat at the picnic table, talking with Moth. All of them got up when they saw her, and Precious ran to give her a hug. Michael and Moth followed behind her.

"Aunt Lucy, may we go visit my father for a while?" Precious asked.

"I've done all my homework," Michael said, answering Lucy's next question before she could ask it. "And Moth says he'll take us through the gate and bring us back."

Lucy looked at Moth. "I'll take good care of them," he assured her.

"I want them back by dinnertime," she said. "*Our* dinnertime, *today*, in two of our hours."

"Very well," Moth agreed.

As they started across the yard to the gate, Lucy added, "and if they're not back by then, I'm coming after them."

"They'll be back on time, Lucy," Moth said fervently. "You have my word."

WEATHER WITCH

It was all Peter's fault. If he hadn't given me *How to Become a Witch in 12 Easy Lessons* for my birthday, none of this would have happened. And he didn't want to weed the vegetable garden yesterday.

Well, maybe some of it was my fault, too. I didn't want to weed the garden either; it's really not a fun way to spend a beautiful Saturday morning. And I am nearly two years older than Peter, and Dad is always saying that a big sister should set a good example for her little brother. And I was the one who looked up at a sky with only a couple of puffy little clouds high up in it and remarked, "Gee, if it were raining, we wouldn't be able to weed the garden."

Peter's face lit up, the way it always does when he gets one of his bright ideas. His "bright" ideas always get us into trouble we could never have imagined when he came up with them, and if I'd had any sense at all I'd have run for the garden and started weeding.

"Jan, I'm pretty sure there's a rain-making spell in that book I gave you."

I guess I don't have much sense, because I followed Peter up to my room and helped him look for the book. He was the one who found it, shoved under my bed with eight other books I'm supposedly reading, including my history textbook and two library books—one overdue, one miraculously not.

As advertised, the book was divided into 12 lessons, and it did say on the first page to do them in order. But Weather Magic was Lesson 7, and we didn't have time to do lessons 1

72

through 6 and still make it start raining before Dad found us goofing off.

So we took the book and went outside to our favorite place down by the stream where we hide when we don't want to do chores. Bruce, our collie, followed us, but he just lay down and went to sleep, so he wasn't in our way. Peter held the book and told me what to say and I cast the spell. I think I did just what the book said to, and Peter says I did, too. And at least part of it must have been right, because it did rain. But, honest, the book said "rain," not "tornado"!

I was standing there with my eyes scrunched closed, concentrating on making it rain, when Bruce started whimpering and scrabbled to his feet. I opened my eyes to see what was bothering him and saw all those dark grey clouds piling up. I yelped, Peter looked up from the book, and the wind hit the tops of the trees with a great rushing roar. We ran for the storm shelter under the barn as fast as we possibly could and made it just as the storm hit. I got pretty wet during the last few seconds before Dad, who had been watching anxiously for us, got the door closed behind me.

Peter was smart enough to hide the book under his shirt before Dad saw it, and Dad was so relieved we were safe that he didn't ask too many questions about where we had been and what we'd been doing that we didn't notice the storm coming sooner.

It was a pretty bad storm, but at least nobody got killed or badly hurt, and most of the crops are okay. But it went straight through the place where we cast the spell, and it only missed our house by about ten yards!

Today is a beautiful day, with not a single cloud in a brilliant blue sky. And as soon as I finish cleaning up the vegetable garden and weeding what's left of it, I'm going to take that book, starting with Lesson 1, and read it very, very carefully.

THINGS THAT GO GRUMP
IN THE NIGHT

Julian Evans let himself in through the back door, collapsed in a chair at the kitchen table, and dropped his schoolbooks on the chair next to him. After fifteen years of living with two highly successful, busy professionals for parents, he knew better than to put anything on the kitchen table unless he had just personally wiped off the table. (He still remembered vividly the look on his fifth grade teacher's face when Julian returned his report card with his mother's signature on the front and orange marmalade on the back.) Feeling thoroughly discouraged, he surveyed the mess around him. It made him feel tired just to look at it. He had skipped lunch, too, but the sight of his mother's kitchen was enough to take away his appetite, regardless of how hungry he'd been before walking in the door. Sighing, he started clearing things up.

He had the kitchen about halfway cleaned up when he heard his mother's car in the driveway. A few seconds later, she breezed in, dropped an armload of papers and magazines on the newly cleared table, and bent to kiss his cheek. "Hi, sweetheart. Did you have a nice day?" Without pause she continued, "Mine was so hectic—and your father and I are going out tonight." She pulled out the hairpins that held her long blond hair in a prim bun and dropped them on the table, shaking her hair loose as she did so. "I did tell you that, didn't I?" She picked up the tea kettle, shook it, took it to the sink to fill it, and put it on the burner.

"I think so," Julian said, "and, anyway, it's on the calendar—dinner with the Witkes and theatre."

"Good." She rummaged around for several minutes, apparently looking for the tea canister, which was on a shelf across the room. The kettle started screaming just as she found it, and she grabbed a mug out of the cupboard, made herself a cup of tea, brought it and a bag of cookies to the table, and buried her nose in a magazine.

Julian silently got up, turned off the burner, picked up the teabag from the stove where she had dropped it, put it in the garbage, put the lid on the canister, and closed the cupboards the mug and the cookies had come from. Then he flopped back into his chair, took a handful of cookies, and began munching moodily on them. His mother, engrossed in her magazine, ignored him. He wondered idly if he were a changeling; he certainly didn't seem to have much in common with his parents. It wasn't just that they were so sloppy and he was neat, but he didn't even look like them. Well, he did have blond hair, like his mother, but his father was dark-haired and both his parents were tall, while Julian was only five foot six. Oh, well, maybe he'd grow some more—assuming they really were his parents.

A few minutes later his father arrived home, set his briefcase and coat on top of Julian's books, and dropped the day's mail on top of the pile already on the table. "You can certainly tell Christmas is coming," he remarked, indicating the two inch pile of catalogs which comprised most of the mail. "How did we get on so many mailing lists, anyway?"

"Because I buy from them," his wife replied. "Where else can you do your shopping between three and four in the morning?"

"How much more stuff do we need—or, for that matter, how much more can we fit in this house?"

She ignored him. "Julian, dear, do you have any ideas as to what you'd like for Christmas?"

Julian, grimly surveying the chaos around him, replied promptly, "A brownie."

His mother looked confused. "One brownie? I think we've got a box of brownie mix around here somewhere—" She looked around vaguely.

"No, Mother," Julian said impatiently. "Not that kind of brownie—the kind that comes in at night and cleans up the place."

He father burst out laughing. "Son, if you can find a brownie willing to work in the mess, you can have it!"

His mother looked hurt. "I know I'm not the world's best housekeeper, Julian, but surely there are more important things in life." She grabbed her tote bag and rummaged in it. "That reminds me; I brought you a present." She produced a box from the local bakery. "Chocolate éclairs, your favorite."

"Thanks, Mom," Julian said. After all, what else could he say?

Half-an-hour later they were gone, but certainly not forgotten—the trail of coats, shoes, socks, and papers led from the back door to their bedroom, and the bathroom floor was hidden beneath a soggy mass of clothes and towels.

Julian made himself a TV dinner—after all, he had to eat something; a guy couldn't live on chocolate éclairs alone. Then he opened the box of éclairs and though hard. Was it brownies you left food out for, or was that only for Santa Claus? Well, it couldn't hurt. Good thing she'd brought him éclairs and not brownies; that would be sort of cannibalistic. He seemed to remember something in the old stories about leaving out a bowl of milk, but that seemed rather insulting to anything in human shape. He compromised by using the widest, lowest glass he could find, and set the glass of milk and an éclair on a cleared spot at the edge of the table. Then he went upstairs to watch television.

He started hearing noises about fifteen minutes later, when he muted the sound during the commercials. He stayed where he was, thinking that if it was a brownie it probably wouldn't want to be disturbed, and a burglar wouldn't be able to find anything in the mess anyway. But about five minutes later, he heard a series of loud bumps that certainly weren't coming from the television, followed by a slamming sound, a loud crash, and an unintelligible curse.

He ran for the head of the stairs and froze. At the bottom of the stairs was a brown little man. It wasn't just that he was dressed in brown, although he was—he was brown all over, skin, hair, and eyes, including the part of the eyes that would have been white on a human. He had a pair of stockings tangled around his ankles, and he was lying amid the fragments of Mrs. Evans's favorite lamp, which had stood on a table at the foot of the stairs.

Julian, forgetting his manners, gave voice to his first reaction. "Oh, no, Mom's gonna kill me!" Then, realizing that this was a very inconsiderate thing to say when the brownie might be seriously injured, he pulled himself together and started down the stairs. "I'm sorry. Are you hurt?"

The brownie held up a commanding hand. "Just a minute, boy." Julian obediently stopped, and watched in surprise as the fragments of the lamp pulled themselves back together, returned to the table, and turned back on. "All right," the brownie continued, "now that you won't cut yourself, come untangle me! What the devil is this thing anyway?"

"Panty hose," said Julian. "Haven't you ever seen them before?"

"Don't get smart with me, boy," snapped the brownie. "How could I have? They must be some new-fangled invention."

"Well, they've been around as long as I can remember, but then I'm not all that old." Julian finished untangling the brownie's legs and held out a hand. "I'm Julian Evans, I'm fifteen, and I'm very happy to meet you."

"I'm sure you are," the brownie said, looking around pointedly. "I'm called Aiken, and I'm 486 years old. What was that thing with the milk?"

"A chocolate éclair," said Julian. "I hope you liked it."

"It will do," said Aiken. "It will do. The important thing for a brownie is to have work to do; the food and milk you leave is just a token of your agreement with the terms. Well, I'd best be about my work—you can go back to whatever you were doing. Pay no mind to the noise." He gathered an armload of clothes and stomped off in the direction of the laundry room. Julian, praying that a brownie's training covered automatic washers and what not to put in them, returned to his television program.

That was Friday night. Saturday morning the house was spotless, and Julian's parents were impressed by his diligence. Of course, it was a wreck again when they went out Saturday night, and when it was spotless Sunday morning, they asked Julian how he was feeling. Julian said, "Just fine," and buried his nose in the comics, ignoring worried whispers about 'obsessive-compulsive behavior.'

He was in his room after dinner when Aiken showed up. "Aren't your parents going out tonight?"

"No, sometimes they do stay home. Can't you work with them here?"

Aiken seemed fascinated by the section of shag carpeting he was stirring with his toe. "Well, it's harder." He looked up at Julian. "They can't see me, of course, but—"

"They can hear you?" Julian asked.

"I'm afraid so. And if they tell me to leave—even if they say that old prayer about ghosties and so forth..."

"Things that go bump in the night?"

"Yes, that one. If they say that—even as a joke—if they say the words, then I have to go and never return." Aiken looked glum. "And there's not all that much demand for brownies these days. So many of us have absolutely nothing to do." He sighed.

Julian chewed thoughtfully on his lower lip. "Don't worry, Aiken; I'll think of something. Can you manage if they're in the den with the television on?"

Aiken nodded. "It might work. Turn it on loud."

Julian promptly went downstairs, grabbed his parents, and demanded that they come keep him company while he watched TV. "It's okay if you bring your work," he pleaded; "I just want you with me."

This, of course, promptly got both his parents upstairs, determined to keep an eye on him. Julian assured them, that no, they hadn't been leaving him along too much, and everything was fine with him, really; he just wanted their company, as long as they were home anyway. He settled down to watch a fairly noisy movie, congratulating himself on the success of his plan. But even the noisiest movie has its quiet moments, and during those the noises from downstairs were, unfortunately, quite audible.

"What was that?" Mr. Evans asked after a series of particularly loud thuds.

Mrs. Evans frowned. "It sounds like an unbalanced load in the washing machine. Julian, are you doing laundry?"

"What? Oh, yes! I'll go check on it. Be right back—you stay here." Julian dashed downstairs and found Aiken. "Can't you be quieter?"

"How silently can you do housework?" Aiken shot back. "I'm doing the best I can!"

"Okay, okay!" Julian sighed. *Are all brownies this noisy?* he wondered. *No wonder so many of them are out of work.* "I'll turn up the volume a bit." He went back to his parents and the movie. There was, of course, no way his parents were going to sit in the same room as a TV with the volume loud enough to drown out the dishwasher being loaded immediately below them. Julian tried desperately to ignore the clank of dishes and prayed, to no avail, that his parents wouldn't notice the noise.

"What's that?" said Mrs. Evans.

"I didn't hear anything," Julian said firmly. There was a loud crash, as if a platter had slipped and broken on the floor.

"And I suppose you didn't hear that, either," said his father. "Don't give me that, Julian, I saw you jump!" He stood up, got his rifle out of the closet, and headed for the door. "I'm going to find out what that is. You stay here."

"No!" Julian shouted horrified. "Dad, put the rifle down!" He ran down the stairs after his father, ignoring his mother's calling after him.

The three of them arrived in the kitchen within seconds of each other. "Freeze!" Mr. Evans yelled. Julian was in time to see Aiken jump and drop a plate, but all his mother saw over his shoulder was the pieces of the plate reassembling and taking their place in the dishwasher.

Aiken glared at Julian and silently mouthed, "Get them out of here." Then he went back to loading the dishwasher. Mrs. Evans fainted.

While his father carried his mother to the nearest couch, Julian grabbed the rifle, ran upstairs, and hid it under the mattress in the guest room. Then he returned with a glass of water. "Here, Dad, give her this."

His father took the water and looked concernedly at Julian. "Son, I think we'd better have a talk."

"Sure, Dad," Julian said. *What choice do I have?* "But can it wait 'til tomorrow? I'm really tired." He faked a yawn.

Mr. Evans silently watched his boots put themselves away in the hall closet. "All right, Julian, tomorrow. But then I want to know what this is all about."

Julian exchanged helpless looks with Aiken and trudged up to bed.

When Julian got to his room after dinner Monday night, he found Aiken sitting on the desk, with the mending piled up next to him. Aiken, looking up from the sock he was darning, asked anxiously, "Are they going to send me away?"

Julian shook his head and flopped onto his bed, now neatly made. "Nope."

Aiken's expression brightened considerably. "Wonderful! What did you tell them?"

"I told them the truth," Julian said. "And I reminded Dad that he said I could have a brownie if I could find one—and you know what?" he asked indignantly. "Not only do they not believe me; they think I'm a poltergeist!"

"A poltergeist!" Aiken's indignation at least equaled Julian's. "Why those—they're daft! Have they ever seen a house a poltergeist's been in?" He was almost screaming with rage, and Julian wondered what his parents were making of this—they must be able to hear it, even if they weren't listening outside his door.

"No, I'm sure they haven't," Julian said hastily, "and neither have I, but I'll bet it looks a lot like the bathroom after they've dressed to go out for the evening."

Aiken looked startled for a minute, then fell over laughing. When he could speak again, he said, "It does, indeed it does." Then he stopped laughing and lowered his voice to a near whisper. "They're not going to bring in a priest and do an exorcism or anything like that, are they?"

"No," said Julian gloomily, "they're sending me to a psychiatrist. There go my Saturday mornings. I don't know what they're so upset about—they're getting the house cleaned and the laundry done! Why do they have to understand it all? Why can't they just be happy with the results?"

"I'm sorry," Aiken said after a moment. Then he added hesitantly. "Do you want me to leave?"

"No!" Julian said quickly. "Don't you dare leave me stuck with having to see a shrink and do the housework on top of it! Besides," he added, "even if you did leave, they already think I'm crazy and I'd still have to see the shrink. You're the only good thing that's happened to me this year—you've got to stay.

"Gladly." It was the first time Julian had seen Aiken smile.

Dr. Leith turned out to be pretty decent, not at all what Julian had expected a psychiatrist to be. He'd expected somebody old and grim and serious, but Dr. Leith was middle-aged, with medium brown hair only half turned grey, and a few extra pounds around her hips, which the loose slacks she wore didn't hide. She was comfortable-looking; in fact, she looked like Julian's idea of what a mother ought to look like. When he told her this, she just smiled and said that she'd started out as a pediatrician and raised four children, so perhaps she'd led a less sheltered existence than most psychiatrists. "Does that bother you?" she asked.

"Just being here bothers me," Julian said. "I'm not crazy, I don't need a shrink, and there are lots of other things I'd rather be doing on Saturday mornings."

"I'm sure there are," she agreed. "Do you know what your parents wanted you to see me?"

"No," he said with mock innocence. "Why?"

"Think about it," she said. "What was happening in your life when they asked you to come see me?"

"Told me to, you mean," he muttered. She seemed okay, and she wasn't giving him a hard time about being a smart-aleck, but he wasn't going to tell anyone else about Aiken. Telling his parents had been quite enough. If he told her, she might think he really was crazy and lock him up somewhere, and he didn't want that. He looked around the room, seeking something safe to talk about. "You have a lot of toys here," he remarked.

"Yes, a lot of my work is with young children."

"Tidy young children, it looks like," Julian said. The room was amazingly neat, especially considering all the stuff in it.

Dr. Leith laughed. "That's because you're my first appointment today. What you see is the way the cleaning service leaves it, not the way it looks after a few hours of being played with."

"Cleaning service?" Julian asked. "Do you mean somebody comes in at night and cleans up?"

"Yes, exactly," Dr. Leith said. "Many office buildings contract with a cleaning service to come in at night and clean."

"When there's nobody here to be bothered by the noise," Julian said slowly. In his mind he could hear Aiken sighing, *So many of us have absolutely nothing to do.* He thought furiously for a minute and then asked, "How does one start a cleaning service?"

"Well, you have to be at least eighteen to start your own business," she began.

"That's okay," Julian said cheerfully. *After all, what do three years matter to people who live for centuries?*

When he arrived home for lunch, both of his parents were waiting for him. "How did it go, dear?" his mother asked, almost before he was through the door.

"Fine," Julian said briefly.

"You seem pretty cheerful," his father observed. "Do you like Dr. Leith?"

"Yeah, she's okay."

"But do you think she'll be able to help you?" his mother asked anxiously.

"Mother," Julian said, "you have no idea how much she's helped me already."

A PRINCE AMONG FROGS

Jan looked into her refrigerator and frowned. "Out of diet soda again," she muttered. "When am I ever going to learn to shop properly?" She closed the refrigerator door and went outside to her back patio.

She decided to go next door to her cousin Julian's house. Julian was 16 years old and a neatness freak. Over the past year, with the help of his decidedly unusual cleaning service, his home had gone from total chaos (courtesy of his absent-minded parents) to a place that could be depended on to have whatever Jan had just run out of. And she knew Julian was home; she could hear him talking to a friend on his patio.

She walked through the gate between their back yards, calling out a greeting to Julian and his friend, just as the sun set.

Since both of them were looking at her, she was the only one who saw exactly what happened next—and even she didn't believe it at first.

There was a flash of bright light, outshining the floodlights which lit the terrace, and a loud popping sound from an aquarium which had been sitting on the terrace next to Julian's friend. When she had opened the gate, the aquarium had contained a frog. Now it was on its side and a naked man was sitting beside it. He looked to be about Jan's age (mid-twenties), and the first thing she noticed as she stared at him was that he was gorgeous. His eyes were brilliant blue, his hair was blond and shoulder length, and his muscles... His pecs looked like something off the cover of a romance novel, but he had the leg muscles of a figure skater. *Of course*, a tiny voice in her mind said, *if he really was just a frog, he would have great legs.*

He also looked disoriented by his surrounding and very embarrassed by his nudity, especially when he noticed Jan staring at him. He blushed and moved quickly to stand behind the nearest chair. Since the chair was wrought iron filigree, it wasn't much cover, but Jan supposed it was the thought that counted. She felt a bit embarrassed herself—it wasn't like her to drool over a man's muscles.

The boys' conversation stopped dead as they twisted in their chairs and saw what Jan was looking at. Julian, his jaw hanging, just stared at the man for a second. Then he found his voice. "Aiken!" he screamed.

The door to the kitchen opened and shut again. "What's wrong, Julian?" a gruff low-pitched voice asked.

"He, uh—" Julian pointed to the naked man.

The man, still clutching the back of the chair, twisted to face the door and inclined his head gravely, looking relieved at the sight of the small brown man.

Stranger and stranger, Jan thought. *He can see Aiken, and he's not freaking out—which is how most people react to him.*

"Good evening, gentlebeing," the man said. "Peace be to the house thou keepest."

"I thank thee, Highness," Aiken replied. "Master Julian," he continued, "I am a brownie. I do floors, I do walls, I do windows, I even do ceilings. I do not, however, do enchanted princes, enchanted frogs, or any combination thereof. You'll have to get help for this little problem elsewhere." The kitchen door closed behind him with a definite snap.

"An enchanted prince?" Julian asked incredulously.

"You have a brownie for a housekeeper?" his friend said in disbelief. "I thought brownies existed only in fairy tales— except for the chocolate kind."

"What's wrong with having a brownie?" the prince asked curiously. "I'm sure he's an excellent housekeeper. And, to be frank, I consider his suggestion that we seek further help an excellent one."

Julian looked helpless. "Jan? Have you got any ideas?"

"Jan?" the prince asked, turning to look at her.

"This is my cousin Jan," Julian explained. "She'll know what to do; she's a witch."

"A witch," his friend repeated. "Your housekeeper is a brownie, and your cousin is a witch. I suppose your aunt is the tooth fairy?"

"Not that I know of," Julian said calmly. "And who are you to talk, Danny?" he added, somewhat less calmly. "You're the one with the enchanted frog prince!"

"He's not my prince—or frog—or whatever," Danny protested. "I never even saw him before last night! Thea brought him to my little sister's slumber party and persuaded Jennifer to kiss him, and then—" he broke off, shaking his head.

"Is your cousin a powerful witch?" the prince asked Julian hopefully.

Julian nodded. "She called up a tornado for her very first spell when she was only eleven."

"Impressive," the prince remarked.

"Maybe," Danny said dubiously. He seemed the most unnerved of them by the whole business. Jan guessed that it was his first exposure to magic. She and Julian had become a bit blasé on the subject. "What was she *trying* to do when she called up the tornado?"

Jan laughed. "I was trying to make it rain so that my brother Peter and I wouldn't have to weed the vegetable garden. I've learned better since then. I'll do what I can, Julian, but I'm due at the theater tonight. Now, what's going on?"

"Well," Julian, belatedly remembering his manners, started with introductions. "This is my friend Danny, and this is—"

As Julian groped for a name he did not know, something seemed to jog the prince's memory. Suddenly he looked a good deal less dazed and confused than he had a moment ago.

"Prince Florian of Astrefiore, at thy service, Mistress." He bowed from behind his chair. Jan got the impression he would have kissed her hand if he could have reached it.

"But when I brought him here," Danny said, pointing to the aquarium, "he was a frog."

"Well," Jan said calmly, dropping into a chair, "why don't we start with getting him some clothes to wear. And, Julian, do you have any diet soda here? I've run out at home."

"Yeah, sure; I'll get some." Julian looked relieved to be dismissed, however temporarily. "You want ice in the soda?"

"Please."

Julian disappeared into the kitchen, and Jan looked at Florian and Danny. "Why don't you sit down," she suggested, "and tell me what happened?"

Danny sat down again, but Florian clearly did not wish to leave the shelter of the chair. He did, however, start talking.

"There was a beautiful young princess named Rowena," he began, "who was abducted by a dragon on her fourteenth birthday."

Danny made a sudden choking noise; Jan glared him into silence.

"My eldest brother was among the guests at the party when she was carried off," Florian continued, "and he came home and told us of her abduction—and of how her own father forbade all of the princes gathered there to attempt her rescue!" He obviously still felt indignant at such injustice and at the king's lack of feeling for his daughter's plight. "As it is the clear duty of a prince to rescue such an innocent victim, and as King Mark's unnatural command was not binding on *me*, I set out for the mountain where the dragon laired." He stopped and frowned. "I remember the journey to the mountain, and I remember approaching the dragon's cave and hearing the most frightful shrieking noise... and the next thing I remember was being in a most strange room with a very soft floor, full of maidens I had never seen before, dressed in odd apparel—" he broke off, eyeing Jan's blue jeans.

"My sister's slumber party," Danny explained, picking up the story. "One of her friends brought him as a sort of joke present—you know, for Jennifer to kiss—but when she did, he turned human, and the girls all started screaming and I came downstairs to see what was happening—I thought he was on drugs, 'cause he looked so spaced out—and then he turned back to a frog again, and my parents came home just then, so I took him upstairs and put him in my old aquarium. I thought maybe I dreamed the whole thing, but I brought him here tonight just in case, and now he's turned human again, and I can't take him home if he's going to keep doing this—my mother will have fits!"

"When?" Jan asked.

"When what?"

"When did he change back to a frog last night?"

Danny frowned and tried to remember exactly, "I think it was about seven-thirty, because it was right before my parents came home." He shuddered. "If they'd come in two minutes earlier, they would have seen him change, and I don't think they'd have liked it. But if they had seen him change," he said, "I don't think Dad would want to take him to school. He teaches biology," he added in explanation for the last remark.

"Seven-thirty," Jan murmured. "I assume that nobody kissed him again or did anything else that might have triggered a change?"

"Not unless you count screaming, running, and hiding behind the furniture," Danny said. "I started to call 911, but when Thea said he'd been a frog, I decided I didn't want to try to explain *that* to the police."

Jan leaned back in her chair, closed her eyes, and tried to concentrate. She had a guilty feeling that part of this was her fault. She was a stage magician, in addition to being a witch, and she had been trying for days to come up with a really good original illusion. Prince Florian's appearance in her life

88

looked like a definite example of "Be careful what you pray for; you will certainly get it."

"Magical transformations," she muttered. "It's not the standard frog prince spell, or a virgin's kiss would have turned him human permanently—I assume your sister is a virgin."

"She'd better be," Danny said grimly. "She's only thirteen."

"Vampires don't turn into frogs," Jan continued to think aloud, "and their transformations are voluntary. Werewolves change at the full moon—"

She looked up at the moon, low in the western sky. "The moon is waxing now. I wonder what time it sets tonight."

Aiken and Julian returned, Julian with a glass of soda, and Aiken with a book, a clipboard and pen, a calculator, and a set of clothes for Florian. He dumped everything but the clothing in front of Jan, then took Florian aside and helped him to dress—Florian had obviously never seen a sweat shirt or sweat pants before and seemed unclear on the concept of underwear. Jan tried not to watch—at least not obviously—and managed to keep from giggling when Florian got tangled in the sweat shirt. Aiken looked as if he wanted to swear, but was restraining himself out of respect for the Prince's rank.

Julian seemed happy to let Aiken handle this problem. He set the soda on the table in front of Jan and flopped into the remaining chair. "How's it going?"

"I'm thinking," Jan said, pausing to sip her soda. She looked at the book Aiken had dropped in front of her. It was an almanac and when she opened it, the pages turned to an explanation of how to calculate moonrise and moonset. Jan grabbed the clipboard and calculator and started figuring. It took about five minutes before she had her answer. The moon had set last night at 7:32 pm local time. "I think it's some sort of crazy cross between the frog prince spell and lycanthropy. If it's a sun-down moon-up transformation, which is my best guess at the moment, he'll turn back to a frog about an hour later tonight than he did last night. We'll need to observe him for a while and find out exactly what time he turns back into a frog."

"Is there no way to stop that from happening, Mistress?" Prince Florian asked, poking his head out of the sweatshirt. "Before I was not aware when I was a frog, but now I am, and I do not enjoy it."

"Not in the next two hours, which is all the time I have now," Jan said briskly. "I've got to be at the theater in time to get ready for my act."

"Thou art an *actress*?" The prince looked scandalized. Obviously where he came from, actress ranked well below witch on the social scale. "Surely a witch does not need to earn her bread displaying herself on the stage like some common harlot."

"No, I'm a stage magician. Don't look so shocked, Prince Florian. I enjoy it, and it pays the bills. You do realize, don't you," she gestured at the house and yard, "that you're not in your own world anymore? We may have a few princess left, but dragons exist only in story tales. And women on the stage," she looked him straight in the eye, "are *not* harlots."

Florian looked around him. "This is indeed a strange world." He looked dismayed. "What can I do here?"

"Maybe you could put him in your act," Danny suggested hopefully. "If you can predict exactly when he's going to change, you can work up a Frog Prince routine, can't you?"

Be careful what you pray for... Jan thought. *Well, at least it was a quick response.*

She chewed on her lower lip and looked upward, calculating furiously. "Let's see: if I'm right about the spell, at moon dark he'd be a frog almost all night; at full moon he'd be human most of the night. The waning moon rises after sunset and doesn't set until after sunrise, so he'd turn human well after dark and frog at dawn, and the waxing moon rises before sunset and sets before dawn, so he'd turn human at sunset. There's too much variation in moonrise, but with daylight savings time I can do the dinner show and use sunset. That changes only about a minute per night. So if I time the act carefully, it should work for at least part of the month. That's not a bad idea, Danny. I take it you weren't planning to keep him as a pet."

"No," Danny said, "My father was planning to take him to school for next week's biology lab."

"That would be a problem," Jan acknowledged. She turned to Florian. "Did you understand what I was saying? Until I can come up with a counter-spell and return you to your own world—neither of which is likely to happen soon, I'm afraid—you are going to be a frog all day and part of most nights. You can live with me—"

"You can have my aquarium," Danny offered.

"Thank you, Danny. You can live in it during the day, Prince Florian, and I'll make sure you have food and water. I live next door, so Julian and Danny can visit you. On nights when the change is at the proper time, you can work in my magic act with me. And I'll keep trying to find a way to free you from the spell and send you back to your own world. Do we have a deal?"

Florian looked at the moon, which was moving steadily toward the horizon.

"Agreed," he said.

Over the next several weeks, Jan studied Florian and the spell he was under. It seemed to be layered: the first layer had turned him into a frog permanently, then, presumably by means of a virgin's kiss, he had gone to the second layer, where he was human part of the time, was able to recover most of his previous human memories, and retained consciousness even when he was in frog form. (He was also becoming addicted to television.) Jan suspected that the spell had at least one, and maybe two, additional layers, but she didn't know what they were or how to trigger them.

While Jan studied Florian, Florian studied her world, beginning with television. Jan made him start watching Sesame Street when she discovered he couldn't read. She sat with him when she could, explaining what was fact, what was sitcom, and what was advertising; and she told the boys to do likewise when they were with him. (She found out later that they were renting videos for him while she was out during the day and was thankful that they were too young to rent anything X-rated.)

Florian liked some of the educational programming, particularly "Mathnet"—changing the channel when that was on brought loud croaks of protest, but mostly he liked CNN or the sports channel, although he found Star Trek (in any form) fascinating. He also developed a taste for opera after stumbling across a performance of "Turandot" one night while channel surfing in human form.

Aiken had produced a wardrobe for him (Jan didn't ask how or where), so toward the end of the month, when he was human late at night, Jan started taking him out with her. They went to a couple of late night movies and did a lot of driving around to get Florian used to the city environment. To Jan's surprise, he seemed to like it. She found it hard to understand how he could adapt so well to such an alien environment.

They also worked out the details of the act, beginning with a costume: a pair of tights of very stretchy material. Aiken provided them, too, which was a good thing, because Jan had no idea where else she could get something that would stretch from frog to human size. Fortunately Prince Florian wasn't very tall, even though his legs were well-muscled. After he'd worn them through a few transformations, Jan got over her initial fear that they'd split right off him, getting them both arrested for indecency. As soon as he changed to human, he added a cloak to the outfit, which made him look much more dressed. Of course, he still looked very sexy.

"The women in the audience are going to love this," Jan said. It was nearing moon dark, which meant they were working during the hours just before dawn. "Now are you sure you remember the patter?"

"Mistress Jan," Florian said patiently, "in my own world I had some slight degree of fame as a minstrel. And where I come from, we are expected to *remember* things, not look them up in a book. He looked pointedly at the almanac Jan was studying as she sat on the floor, surrounded by several reference books, a calculator, a pen, and a lot of paper.

"It is very important that we get sunset and moonrise and moonset times correct," Jan said. "That's the key to our act. Actually, timing is vital in most magic."

"I understand that," Florian said. "The boys brought some videotapes for me to watch. I trust thou dost not plan to saw me in half."

"No," Jan said. "I'm not very fond of that trick. I saw a show in Las Vegas once where they must have done at least three variations of the 'saw-the-woman-in-half trick' and I would have walked out if it had been possible. Unfortunately I was stuck at a table in a dark room, surrounded by people I would have had to crawl over. Besides, I was with my aunt and uncle, who would have thought it ill-mannered of me to leave in the middle of a show. There were only about three good illusions, which is *not* enough to carry a two-hour show. I have rarely been so bored in my life. That's one of the reasons I keep my act short."

Florian sighed. "I am glad my father is not here to see this. He would not approve at all."

Jan looked up at Florian. He was sprawled in an armchair, wearing only his tights. They were bright blue and matched his eyes, but she doubted that his father would appreciate the effect. "I'm sure you're correct," she said, "and I'm glad he's not here too."

Florian smiled suddenly at her. It was a smile to make a woman's knees quiver. *What is his world like that he had to take on a dragon to find a woman?* Jan wondered. *Even though he was a surplus prince, there should have been some girl who would want him.*

"I think my father would like thee," he said.

"Really?" Jan raised her eyebrows. "As much as Princess Rowena?"

"Better than Princess Rowena," Florian said. "Thou hast a good heart and a strong sense of honor. That is more important than being the daughter of a king."

"What is she like?" Jan asked. This was the first time the subject had come up since the night she met Florian. "Is she very beautiful?"

"Princesses with large dowries are beautiful by definition," Florian said with a slight tinge of cynicism in his tone. "In fact, I did not see much of her, and what I did see—" he smiled. "I am quite content not to have married her, even if being a frog is part of the price of escaping that fate." He smiled again at Jan. "Thou dost outshine her in beauty as the sun does the moon."

"Uh, thanks," Jan said, suddenly feeling awkward. "You're pretty good-looking too." She bent her head over the almanac again. "Now if the moon sets at 16:56 at 40 degrees North Latitude at the Greenwich Meridian, it will set at—" she put the calculator on top of the almanac and punched numbers into it with her left hand while making notes on a pad of paper with her right. "—20:30 local time here. That gives us plenty of time to do the act. We can start next week."

"Canst thou not tell with thy true magic when the transformation is about to take place?" asked Florian. "I can feel when it is to happen."

Now that he mentioned it, Jan realized that she could tell. "You're right, she said. "You look sort of fuzzy for a few seconds right before it happens. That's how I know when to kiss you so that it looks as if my kiss is turning you human. But it's only a few seconds' warning, and I have to be watching for it. That's why all the calculations are necessary. I *really* don't want anything to go wrong with this on stage."

"Nothing will," Florian reassured her. "Thou hast calculated the times for the next two months, thy costume is done and looks wonderful, and I know exactly what I'm to do for the tricks after I turn human when I act as thine assistant. We are going to do well, believe me."

Florian was correct. The new act was a smash hit, and the audience for the dinner show increased dramatically over the next two weeks. But as the full moon approached, when moonrise would come after sunset, Jan told the manager that she would not be able to perform for a couple of weeks. He protested vigorously, and she agreed to one more show, on the night of the full moon, before taking a break. Given this concession, he readily agreed to schedule her an hour later than usual. Jan spent most of the day pacing about the house, checking and double-checking the local time for moon rise, and talking anxiously to a frog whose side of the conversation was limited, to say the least.

The house was packed, and Jan was a nervous wreck. She ran her hands over the skirt of her long blue dress, which was a perfect match for Florian's tights and cape, redid her hair twice, double-checked her make-up, and triple-checked her props.

"I still have a bad feeling about this," she told Florian as she carried his box to the stage. "I keep thinking that I forgot something important."

Once she started the familiar tricks that began her act, she found herself relaxing. The first part of the act was simple slight-of-hand, things she had been doing since her early teens, showy, but not difficult. Now, of course, they served to fill in the time until the proper moment for Florian's transformation.

As moonrise approached, she brought Florian out of his box and began to tell the story of how her poor assistant had encountered a dragon who had put him under an evil spell, which could be broken only by a maiden's kiss. She watched Florian carefully as she spoke, waiting for the right moment. To her relief, her timing was perfect, and the transformation went as smoothly as it had when they had been using sundown as the mark for it.

Jan relaxed now, prepared to run the rest of the act normally. But when they were almost at the end of the act, Florian suddenly nudged her, and she saw the shimmer that always proceeded his transformation. As the flash of light momentarily blinded her (she had failed to close her eyes as she usually did), she suddenly remembered the one thing she had forgotten to check in her calculations. *Lunar eclipses occur at the full moon.*

She could see again, but she was looking at a cape on the floor beside her. She bent and lifted it off Florian, whom she picked up and held in the palm of her hand, turning her head towards the audience. A roomful of wide-eyed people stared at them, and Jan said the first thing that came into her mind. "Have you ever noticed how hard it is to get good help these days?"

That got a laugh from the audience and served to convince them that this was all part of the show. Now all Jan had to do was find a plausible way to finish off the act.

Is this an eclipse? If it is, how long is it going to last? She watched anxiously for any sign that Florian was going to change back, but he seemed solidly frog.

"Kiss him again!" a woman called from the audience. "Remember that love conquers all."

"I wish I believed that," Jan whispered to Florian. "Still, I suppose it's worth a try. Be human!" She leaned her face toward his.

Florian suddenly tensed in her hand, jumped forward, and touched his lips to hers. There was another blinding flash of light, right in her face, and a heavy weight pushed her arm to her side. Before her vision cleared, she was swept off her feet into a man's arms, and when she could see again she was cradled against Florian's bare chest, her arms wrapped about his neck for balance. She tightened her grip reflexively as he bowed to the audience, still holding her, even though his grasp on her was quite secure.

"True it is indeed that love conquers all," he said. "I have loved my lady here from the day I met her, and our love has freed me from the dragon's spell." He set Jan carefully on her feet and knelt before her, taking both her hands in his. "My lady, wilt thou marry me?"

What a great sense of theater! Jan thought, nodding her head. Under the circumstances, she could hardly say no, and she was too stunned to speak anyway. The audience cheered loudly as Jan and Florian took their bows and Florian swept her into his arms again and carried her offstage.

They had barely reached their dressing room when the manager burst in. "Great ending!" he exclaimed. "We'll have no problem giving you a couple of weeks off now—we can say you're on your honeymoon. Or maybe you should get married on stage here—what do you think?"

Jan finally found her voice. "I think we should go home and discuss the details," she said. "This was a little sudden." She smiled shyly at Florian, who put a protective arm around her shoulders.

"Of course," the manager said. "Give me a call in the morning. Oh, congratulations."

"Thank you," Florian said gravely.

They were both silent as they changed to street clothes and loaded the props into Jan's car. Jan had a lot of questions, but she certainly wasn't going to ask any of them until they were safely home.

As soon as she was inside the house, Jan grabbed the almanac, sat down on the sofa, and looked up lunar eclipses. She frowned in bewilderment. "I thought it must have been an eclipse," she told Florian, "that made you change back during the act, and there was an eclipse today, but it was only partial and hours before we even started the show. I don't understand."

Florian sat down beside her and put his arm around her. "I have seen many thing I do not understand," he said. "But I understand that I love thee—perhaps the lady who said that love conquers all was correct."

"That was a great line, asking me to marry you," Jan said. "You really saved the show tonight; I just about froze up when you turned back into a frog."

"That was not a line," Florian said firmly. "I would be greatly honored if thou wouldst consent to be my wife."

Jan started to shake her head, more in disbelief than anything else, and Florian pressed his fingers to her lips. "Do not give me thine answer now," he said quietly. "Take time to consider it."

"Don't you think we should figure out what happened first?" Jan asked.

"No. I think the first thing thou shouldst do is go to bed and get some sleep. It has been a long day for thee." He picked her up again and carried her to her bedroom. Jan was too tired to protest, and she discovered that she rather liked being carried about. There was something oddly reassuring about it.

But when Florian set her on her bed, lay down beside her and began to nuzzle on her neck, Jan decided that this was not a good time to let her hormones override her brain. "Florian," she said firmly, "there *are* worse things than being a frog."

Either the threat worked, or Florian's sense of chivalry prevailed. He dropped one final chaste kiss on her cheek and left the room.

Jan got up long enough to strip off her clothes and put on a nightgown and then fell asleep the second she got back into bed.

When she woke again it was mid-morning and the sun was streaming in through her window. She threw some clothes on and headed for the kitchen, calling a greeting to Florian as she passed through the living room. But instead of the usual croak from the aquarium, the reply came from a human sitting on the sofa. Jan stopped in her tracks and stared, then narrowed her eyes to use her other sight.

"Looks like the spell's gone to another layer," she informed him. "We'll have to work out the new parameters."

"I have been working with it since dawn," he replied. "It seems to be under voluntary control."

"What?" Jan asked in astonishment. There was the usual flash of light, and a frog sat on her sofa, looking at her expectantly. She walked over, knelt beside it, closed her eyes, and kissed it, keeping her eyes closed. She had been temporarily blinded quite enough the night before. When she opened her eyes again, Florian was in human form.

"I can do it whether thou dost kiss me or no," he explained, "but now we do not have to worry about timing the kiss so precisely."

"We'll have to wait a day or so to be sure that the spell isn't influenced by the sun or moon," Jan said cautiously, "but if you can control it, we can do the act anytime."

Then she realized what this meant to Florian, rather than to her magic act. "You can be human all the time if you wish now," she said. "You don't have to turn into a frog, if you don't want to." She forced herself to smile. "I'm really happy for you."

"But something troubles thee," Florian said.

"Well, it was definitely the best magic act I ever had." *I'm not going to cry*, Jan told herself firmly. *He is a sentient being with a right to his own life—he is not my property.*

"I have become quite comfortable being a frog," Florian said. "I do not mind at all doing it professionally, so long as I can be human when I wish."

Jan nodded. "That was the first half of my part of the bargain. Now all I have to do is figure out a way to send you home."

I don't want to send you anywhere, she realized suddenly. *I don't want to lose you. I love you. But I did promise, and I keep my promises.*

Florian bent his head and kissed her. To Jan's relief he remained in human form—she had been half-afraid that if he kissed her again he'd turn back into a frog. "My love," he said firmly, "I am home."

ABOUT THE AUTHOR

Elisabeth Waters sold her first short story in 1980 to Marion Zimmer Bradley for THE KEEPER'S PRICE, the first of the Darkover anthologies. She then went on to sell dozens of short stories to a variety of anthologies. Her first novel, a fantasy called CHANGING FATE, was awarded the 1989 Gryphon Award. She is now working on a sequel to it, in addition to her short story writing and anthology editing.

She has also worked as a supernumerary with the San Francisco Opera, where she appeared in *La Gioconda*, *Manon Lescaut*, *Madama Butterfly*, *Khovanschina*, *Das Rheingold*, *Werther*, and *Idomeneo*.

www.ingramcontent.com/pod-product-compliance
Lightning Source LLC
Chambersburg PA
CBHW051308170626
46809CB00004B/1810